Scandinavian Music: A Short History

Scandinavian Music:
A Short History

*

JOHN HORTON

GREENWOOD PRESS, PUBLISHERS
WESTPORT, CONNECTICUT

Library of Congress Cataloging in Publication Data

Horton, John.
   Scandinavian music.

    Reprint of the ed. published by Norton, New York.
    Bibliography: p.
    Includes index.
    1. Music, Scandinavian--History and criticism.
I. Title.
[ML310.H67 1975]   780'.948   73-7673
ISBN 0-8371-6944-5

38,221

Originally published in 1963 by W. W. Norton & Company, Inc.
New York

Reprinted with the permission of John Horton.

Reprinted in 1975 by Greenwood Press, Inc.
51 Riverside Avenue, Westport, CT 06880

Library of Congress catalog card number 73-7673
ISBN 0-8371-6944-5

Printed in the United States of America

10 9 8 7 6 5 4 3 2

Preface

In order to keep the later chapters of this book within reasonable bounds I have thought it expedient to end the survey halfway through the present century. For this reason few references, or none at all, have been made to certain younger Scandinavian composers whose names have been much to the fore during the nineteen-sixties, and important recent works by some well-established composers have also had to be passed over without mention. A few exceptions to this general principle will be found, and where possible the reader's attention has been drawn, in text or footnotes, to biographical and critical studies published after as well as before 1950.

My warmest thanks are due to the many friends and correspondents who have replied to inquiries, made helpful suggestions, and in many cases lent or given documentary material. I should like to name in particular:

Dr. Nils Afzelius, Dr. Walter Bergmann, Mr. Dan Fog, Mr. R. D. Gibson and the staff of Messrs. J. and W. Chester Ltd., Mr. Robert Layton, Mr. Richard Newnham, Mr. Donald Mitchell, Mr. M. Kay-Larsen of the Danish Institute in Edinburgh and the staff of the Royal Danish Embassy in London, Mr. H. E. Saether of the Royal Norwegian Embassy, Dr. P. A. Hildeman and his colleagues in the Swedish Institute for Cultural Relations, Mrs. Tahtinen of the Finnish Legation, Mr. Patrick Saul and the staff of the British Institute of Recorded Sound, Mr. F. Backer-Grøndahl, Dr. P. Krömer, Dr. Kristian Lange and Dr. H. Huldt Nystrøm with other members of the staff of the Norwegian Broadcasting Corporation, Mrs. H. Rieber-Mohn of the Bergen Public Library, Dr. Sevåg of the

7

Oslo Folk Museum, and Dr. Ø. Gaukstad of the Oslo University Library.

I am also indebted to the following public bodies for information and documents readily supplied:

In Copenhagen, the Royal Library, the Arnamagnaean Collection, the National Museum, the Rosenborg Palace, and the Officers' Academy in Frederiksberg Castle; in Hillerød, the National Historical Museum; in Stockholm, the Royal Library, the National Museum, and the Municipal Museum; in London, the British Museum and Cecil Sharp House.

To members of the staff of the Norwegian Office for Cultural Relations and to our friends in Norway my wife and I wish to express our appreciation of the hospitality they have so generously bestowed upon us: among the many to whom we are deeply grateful are Mr. and Mrs. Egil Nordsjø, Mr. and Mrs. Gunnar Saevig, Mr. and Mrs. Harald Saeverud, Mr. and Mrs. Geirr Tveitt, Mr. Ivar Benum, and Mr. Alf Hurum. We remember with gratitude our meetings and conversations with Dr. O. M. Sandvik, Mr. D. Monrad Johansen, and Professor O. Gurvin.

I owe a particular debt to Dr. Gerald Abraham for his constant encouragement, kindly and constructive criticism, and wise and experienced counsel.

Finally, I would thank Mr. Giles de la Mare and the editorial and production staffs of Messrs. Faber and Faber for their interest in this book at every stage of its publication.

JOHN HORTON

January 1963

Contents

Illustrations

ILLUSTRATIONS

I

Pre-Christian and Mediaeval Periods

The earliest traces of music among the Scandinavian peoples show that, as in other primitive communities, the sounds of human voices and instruments were regarded not merely as serving the everyday purposes of communication and signalling in peace and war, but also as possessing supernatural powers associated with the observance of rites and ceremonies and with the preservation and transmission of tribal lore. Our knowledge of these matters is derived from three sources: literary references, pictorial representations of instruments—chiefly in wood and stone—and the remains of actual instruments brought to light by fortunate chance or in the course of archaeological investigations.

The English housewife who buys Danish butter may find that the wrapper bears a minute but accurate drawing of a pair of Bronze Age *lurs* or natural trumpets.[1] To see the originals one must visit the museums of Copenhagen, Stockholm, Oslo, and Stavanger, which among them house the thirty-odd specimens unearthed since the end of the eighteenth century in the Scandinavian peninsula and Northern Germany. They date from at least four hundred years before the Christian era, and both in appearance and sound are among the most splendid relics of the past. The bronze conical tube of the *lur* varies between five and eight feet in length, and is gracefully curved, sometimes in two directions; it terminates in a flattened bell adorned with bosses, and is fitted with a cup-shaped mouthpiece similar to that of the modern trombone. On the best-preserved examples a brass-

[1] The *lur* appears to be depicted among the rock-carvings at Tessen in Beitstad (Norway) and in Bohuslän and Skåne (Sweden).

player can produce the first twelve notes of the harmonic series. The fact that some of these instruments have been found in pairs, symmetrically curved in opposite directions, has encouraged the theory that they were played together, in the manner shown in the group of statuary outside the Copenhagen Town Hall, or demonstrated on replicas by the band-boys in the Tivoli Gardens. If the Bronze Age musicians performed in duet fashion they can hardly have avoided discovering harmonic intervals such as the major third and perfect fourth and fifth, and thus taking at least a step or two towards elementary polyphony and what Curt Sachs called 'the road to major'.[1]

Reliable evidence about the development of stringed instruments first occurs in the sixth century of the Christian era, when the Scandinavian lands were still almost entirely pagan. Two distinct forms of the harp had evolved: the triangular and the round or oblong, the latter often resembling the Graeco-Roman *cithara* and perhaps being the ancestor of two regional instruments that survived until comparatively modern times—the Welsh *crwth* and the Esthonian *tallharpa*. The sixth-century Bishop Venantius Fortunatus associates different varieties of stringed instrument with particular races:

> *Romanusque lyra plaudat tibi, Barbarus harpa,*
> *Graecus achilliaca, chrotta Britanna canat.*

'Let the Roman praise thee with the lyre, the barbarian with the harp, the Greek with the cithara, and let the British *chrotta* resound.'

The obvious inference is that the *chrotta* was the oblong harp, and the triangular shape was used by the non-Christian barbarians of Northern Europe, but the nomenclature of these instruments is very much confused;[2] thus Martin Gerbert, the eighteenth-century author of the treatise *De cantu et musica sacra*, distinguishes the round lyre as *cythara teutonica*, whereas he calls the triangular form *cythara anglica*. Judging by surviving representations and remains, it was the round or oblong harp that the

---

[1] Sachs, C., *The Rise of Music in the Ancient World*, pp. 295 seq., London, 1944.

[2] See Hayes, Gerald, 'Musical Instruments', *New Oxford History of Music*, Vol. III, London, 1960, ch. XIII; also Panum, H., *The Stringed Instruments of the Middle Ages*, revised and edited J. Pulver, London, 1941.

Ia Bronze Age *lur*; National
Museum, Copenhagen

Ib Carved doorpost from church at
Hylestad, Norway (ca. 1200), depicting the story of Gunnar. The episode
of Gunnar's harp-playing in the
serpents' den is at the top

II *Nobilis, humilis*: two-part hymn to St. Magnus; from the thirteenth-century *Codex upsaliensis* (C233)

Scandinavian races knew best: it figures in wood-carvings in the churches of Austad and Hylestad (both in Norway),[1] and fragments of a similar instrument, dating from about A.D. 1300, found at Kravik in Numedal. The Kravik harp appears to have had six strings, like the sixth-century Saxon instrument of different pattern recovered from the Sutton Hoo ship burial in 1939 and now shown in reconstructed form in the British Museum. The persistence of six strings suggests a pentatonic tuning, and it has been suggested that the tuning of the understrings of the much later Hardanger fiddle may preserve a traditional harp-scale.[2]

Apart from illustrating the round harp, the Norwegian church carvings show how strongly the art of harp-playing was linked with magic and myth. The theme in both these examples of intricate and beautiful wood-carving, which date from the twelfth century, is the story of Gunnar Gjukeson in the *Volsung-saga*. Gunnar was thrown into a den of serpents, together with his harp; his hands were bound, but by plucking the harp-strings with his toes he charmed the creatures into docility. Legend surrounds the very origin of another member of the harp family, the *kantele*, a psaltery-like instrument with five strings that found its way into the Scandinavian peninsula during the Middle Ages and became naturalized in Finland, where it is still in use as a popular and educational instrument. The Finnish epic, *Kalevala*, describes how the hero Väinämöinen first made it from the bones of a large pike, and later rebuilt it with birch wood strung with a maiden's hair. Like Orpheus, he enchants all living things with his playing.[3]

These legendary tales, however fanciful, reveal the existence of a tradition of purely instrumental music; and it is remarkable how often this tradition is referred to in Scandinavian literature, and how seldom the sagas treat harp-playing as merely an accompaniment to song. Familiar as we are with the eighth-century Northumbrian St. Bede's vivid account of singing to the harp in the story of Caedmon—and Aelfred's translation

---

[1] See Plate Ib.
[2] See p. 94.
[3] *Kalevala*, trans. W. F. Kirby, London, 1907, runos XL, XLI and XLIV. The *kantele* is to be distinguished from the *kanteleharpa*, which is similar to the Swedish *tallharpa* already mentioned. See Plate XIII.

puts the matter beyond doubt with the phrase *be hearpan singan*—
we might expect similar descriptions in the Norse Eddas and
sagas. In Norse literature, however, harp-playing (*harpasláttr*)
is nearly always a separate art from singing or chanting, for
which the usual word is *kveda*. From the fourteenth-century
sagas we learn that the expert harpist had a repertory of pieces
known by their titles; thus *Nornagespáttr* tells how an itinerant
musician entertained King Olaf Trygvason at Trondheim with
several tunes named after the legendary Gunnar's exploits as a
harpist, and in the *Bosesaga* a virtuoso plays a succession of
tunes, all named, at a wedding party, to such effect that not
only the guests dance, but also the knives and platters. Besides
the outstanding performances of professional musicians, the
skill of distinguished amateurs is commemorated; a passage in
the *Orkneyinga saga* contains verses by Earl Ragnvald Kali
(1135–58) in which he claims

> ... nine accomplishments: a good memory for runes, being
> frequently occupied with books or with building, being skilful
> at skating, being able to shoot and row as occasion demands,
> and understanding the two arts of harp-playing and verse-
> making.

This list may not be untypical of the cultured Norse aristocracy
of Iceland and the Scottish islands in the twelfth century; but
references to a comparatively advanced musical development in
the *Elder* (or *Poetic*) *Edda* and *Heimskringla*, both written down
by the Icelander, Snorre Sturleson (1170–1241), and containing
the stories of the Norse kings, must be treated with some reserve,
as they may represent an idealized picture of the Viking age
and the earliest period of northern Christianity.

The oldest extant Norse poetry embodied in the *Elder Edda*
belongs to the tradition of accentual and alliterative verse
through which the common lore of the northern Germanic
nations was preserved and handed on. Much of it goes back
to the pre-Christian age (before A.D. 1000) and both in metrical
form and poetic imagery has a great deal in common with the
eighth-century English epic of *Beowulf*. At the time when Snorre
lived and made his great compilations, however, the older
literary traditions were beginning to be supplanted by a more
intricate and self-conscious art, that of the court poets or *skalds*.

Skaldic poetry made rapid headway in the early years of the tenth century, when many men of high birth and intellectual ability left Norway in protest against the autocratic rule of Harald Fairhair (860–933) and settled in Iceland, which soon gained a cultural ascendancy over the mother country, and eventually became the chief guardian of mediaeval Norse literature.

While we can know little that is certain about the musical declamation used by the skaldic poets or by the Icelandic communities in reciting the Eddic poems and the newer court verses, a tenuous survival of their practice may exist in the Icelandic tunes written down in the late eighteenth century by Johan Hartmann the elder, probably from the singing of Icelanders visiting or residing in Copenhagen, and published in J. B. de la Borde's *Essai sur la musique ancienne et moderne* (1780). The five melodies—or rather four, for one is given twice—are set to scraps of skaldic verse, and one is described as the tune to which the Eddic *Voluspaa* was still being chanted in eighteenth-century Iceland. *Voluspaa* (or *Vølvespå*) means 'the Sibyl's Prophecy', and forms part of the *Poetic Edda* that probably originated in the tenth century. The following, with some corrections of the Norse text, is the chant as de la Borde prints it:

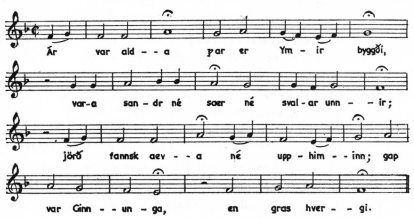

('In the beginning, when Ymir lived, there was neither sand nor sea nor cold waves, nor could any earth or heaven be found; there was Ginnunga, the void, but grass nowhere.')

Another trace of epic or, more probably, skaldic chant may be preserved in the two-part hymn *Nobilis, humilis*, dedicated to the memory of St. Magnus, Earl of Orkney (d. 1115). This primitive but remarkably euphonious example of what was later to be called *gymel* in English manuscripts of the fifteenth century occurs in a manuscript believed to have been written in the Orkneys during the thirteenth century; it is now in the university library at Uppsala.[1]

Nobilis, humilis, Magne martyr stabilis,
Habilis, utilis, comes venerabilis,
Et tutor laudabilis Tuos subditos
serva carnis fragilis mole positos.

('Noble, lowly, Magnus the steadfast martyr, able, serviceable, reverend earl and honoured guardian: save thy people burdened with frail flesh.')

The accentual Latin of the verses is not unlike some of the skaldic metres, and the whole composition has a popular flavour that suggests a secular, perhaps a non-Christian origin. It is possible that this virile hymn, celebrating the virtues of an

---

[1] *Codex upsaliensis* (C 233): see Plate II. The musical importance of this manuscript was first realized by Olaf Kolsrud and Georg Reiss in 1912. The most recent study of the Magnus-hymn is that of Nils L. Wallin in *Svensk Tidskrift för Musikforskning* (*Studier tillägnade Carl-Allan Moberg*), Stockholm, 1961. Wallin argues that the hymn may have been composed as early as 1140, and suggests that it may have been sung at the consecration of St. Magnus Cathedral, Kirkwall, by members of the Earl's family, Latin words being fitted for this solemn occasion to a melody in popular circulation, and sung in parts according to the practice described by Giraldus Cambrensis.

Orkneyan Christian earl, may have been adapted from a heroic lay of pagan times, and that the lower voice-part may be a traditional melody.

The polyphonic setting raises other questions. Almost contemporary with the Magnus-hymn is the famous account of popular part-singing in the *Itinerary of Gerald de Barri* (Giraldus Cambrensis, *c.* 1147–1220).[1] Gerald distinguishes between the free polyphony of the Welsh singers of his day and the more restricted part-singing to be heard 'in the northern district of Britain beyond the Humber and on the borders of Yorkshire'. This northern manner of harmonic extemporization was inherited, he believes, 'from the Danes and Norwegians, by whom these parts of the island were more frequently invaded, and held longer under their dominion'; thus, Gerald surmises, the English, picked up not only the Norsemen's speech but also their way of singing. The description is not precise enough to show whether the Northern practice took the form of harmonization mainly in thirds, as in the Magnus-hymn; it is clear only that the singing was always in two parts, and some kind of parallel movement is suggested. In the more remote Norse colony of Iceland the custom of singing in parallel fifths (*tvísyngja*), as in the mediaeval *organum*, was firmly established by the beginning of the fourteenth century, when it was condemned by Laurentius, Bishop of Hólar but survived almost into modern times. Taken together, these facts indicate that the Scandinavian world played some part in the development of polyphony along the lines of popular, spontaneous improvisation. How far that development had gone by the early years of the thirteenth century is apparent from the supreme masterpiece of secular polyphony, *Sumer is icumen in*, which is contemporary with the Uppsala manuscript of the Magnus-hymn and with Gerald's *Itinerary*.[2]

At its zenith in the tenth century, the Scandinavian empire stretched from Greenland to the heart of European Russia, and included a large part of the British Isles; and this vast expansion of the pagan North was in itself the means of bringing

---

[1] The relevant passages of the Latin text, with English translation, are given in the *New Oxford History of Music*, Vol. II, pp. 315–16.

[2] For the *Reading Rota* and its relationship to popular and learned polyphony, see the *New Oxford History of Music*, Vol. II, p. 402, and Vol. III, p. 109.

Scandinavia within the bounds of Christendom. Missionaries came from southern and western Europe; the pioneer work of St. Willebrod of Northumbria in the eighth century, and of St. Ansgar in the ninth, bore fruit when, in 960, King Harald Bluetooth of Denmark was baptized by the Archbishop of Bremen and ordered bishoprics to be founded in the Danish towns of Slesvig, Ribe and Aarhus. In 1008 Olof the Lap-King became the first Christian king of the Swedes, and in 1030 Olav II, who had spread the faith in Norway with fire and sword, fell in battle at Stiklestad; his body was buried on the site of the future cathedral of Nidaros (now Trondheim) and he was canonized as a martyr king in the following year. Half a century later the Danes also had their royal saint when Canute the Holy, grand-nephew of Canute the Great, was buried in the crypt of Odense cathedral and canonized. In the twelfth century archbishoprics were established at Nidaros (1153) and Uppsala (1164), and the same century saw the rise of the Cistercian monasteries in Sweden. 'The date 1100 is an epoch. . . . It was then that the wandering of the German nations was completed. . . . The Northern world before 1100 was still in great part the world of the *Germania* . . . after 1100 *Germania* is harmonized in the new conception of Christendom.'[1]

Far from checking the creative vigour of its new converts, the Christian religion gave fresh impetus to Norse architecture and the decorative arts, poetry, and song. The genius of the northern races for absorbing cultural ideas from other regions, while retaining and even intensifying their native originality, showed itself in the reconciliation of much that was vital in the old paganism with the Christian attitude to life as it was taught by priests and monks from Britain, France, and Italy. On the sites of the great heathen shrines at Nidaros and Uppsala rose churches, at first of wood but soon of stone, that gave new expression to the ancient fantasies of plant and beast. The northern church was literally a church militant, and as its early saints, like Olav and Canute, were often men of battle, so the hymns that celebrated their prowess and their piety followed the pattern of the pagan hero-songs; and the war-chant of Olav's army at Stiklestad:

---

[1] Ker, W. P., *The Dark Ages*, London, 1904, reptd. 1955, p. 5.

Fram, fram, Kristsmenn, Krossmenn, Konungsmenn
('Forward, men of Christ, men of the Cross, men of the King')

must have resembled the din of the Germanic warriors described by Tacitus in the first century of the Christian era. Some of the songs quoted in *Heimskringla* as having been extemporized by Olav's skalds and 'immediately got by heart by the army' are frankly pagan in language and sentiment.[1]

One of the problems of the early missionaries must have been that of teaching Gregorian plainsong to northern clerics. Visitors to Scandinavia in the period immediately before the introduction of the new faith vie with one another in their uncomplimentary remarks on native singing. The tenth-century Arabian traveller, Ibrahim ibn Ahmed at-Tartushi, describes the ritual singing of the heathen inhabitants of Slesvig as 'a growling that issues from their throats like the baying of hounds, but even more bestial';[2] and the eleventh-century chronicler Adam of Bremen, giving an account of the hideous sacrificial offerings displayed at Uppsala, says that the songs accompanying them were too obscene to dwell upon.[3] Yet in this also the Church eventually triumphed. While pagan songs were adapted as far as possible to Christian use, like the war-song of Olav's army, the converts' ears and throat became gradually accustomed to the chants prescribed by Rome. The contrast between the new rites and the old ceremonial is brought out in a passage in *Heimskringla*, describing how Olav Trygvason turned a meeting for pagan sacrifice into an enforced baptism:

> The following morning, when the king was dressed, he had the early mass sung before him; and when the mass was over, ordered the trumpets to sound for a conference.[4]

Heimskringla also relates how Sigurd Slembedegn, while being tortured to death, 'spoke until he gave up the ghost, and sang between whiles a third part of the psalter, which [was]

[1] *Heimskringla*, trans. Samuel Lane (London, 1844), Everyman edtn. pp. 372 seq.
[2] Quoted in Brøndsted, J., *The Vikings*, London, 1960, p. 40.
[3] Ibid., p. 265.
[4] *Heimskringla*, trans. Lane, p. 62. The Norse text reads: '. . . lét hann syngja sér tiðir, ok er messu var lokit, pá lét konungr blása til húspings.'

considered beyond the powers and strength of ordinary men'.[1] Another episode from the saga of Olaf Trygvason describes the service in Nidaros cathedral at Michaelmas, 999, when a number of pagan Icelanders of consequence were visiting the town:

> When Michaelmas came . . . the king had high mass sung with great splendour. The Icelanders went there, and listened to the fine singing and the sound of the bells; and when they came back to their ships every man told his opinion of the Christian man's worship. Kiartan expressed his pleasure at it, but most of the others scoffed at it. . . .[2]

Before long the parent stock of Latin chant and hymnody put out fresh shoots in the northern climate, and native poets and musicians produced compositions on the model of the hymns and sequences current in the great musical centres of the Church, such as St. Gall, Paris, and Cambrai. Young men were sent from the Scandinavian lands to study in these places, while experts were imported to train native singers for the new cathedrals and collegiate churches. Even far-off Iceland had a French teacher of Church song, a monk whose name was recorded as Richini or Rikinni; he was installed by Bishop Jón of Hólar at the beginning of the twelfth century to teach in the cathedral school.[3]

The oldest complete musical documents from Denmark[4] are three Latin sequences contained in a parchment codex[5] written in the reign of Valdemar I (1157–1182), conqueror of the heathen Wends, whose religious counsellor and companion on the battlefield was Absalon, Archbishop of Lund—then under Danish rule—the founder of Copenhagen. The sequences are of French origin, and point to the influence of Paris on Danish religious life at this time. Of greater national interest, however, is the ritual for the office of St. Canute (Knut Lavard), the father of Valdemar I. It was Canute who endowed the church (afterwards the cathedral) at Lund in 1104, providing for the

[1] *The Norse King Sagas*, trans. Lane, Everyman edtn., p. 355.
[2] *Heimskringla*, p. 73.
[3] For further information on music in mediaeval Iceland, see the article 'Island' in Blume, *Die Musik in Geschichte und Gegenwart*, 1957.
[4] Hammerich, Angul, *Mediaeval Musical Relics of Denmark*, Leipzig, 1912.
[5] *Liber Daticus Lundensis*.

maintenance of a choir; and from these beginnings Lund grew into an important centre of church music. The Council of Lund, summoned by Absalon in 1188, was attended by six Danish bishops; it decided upon forms of ritual and ordered a breviary to be drawn up. The office of St. Canute occurs in a manuscript probably written at Ringsted or Roskilde in the late thirteenth century and now in the university library at Kiel.[1] The ritual includes a hymn, *Gaudet mater ecclesia*, with two melodies, the first of which is in the major mode and suggests a popular origin or intention. There are also two sequences—*Preciosa mors sanctorum* and *Diem festum veneremur*—which are found only in Danish sources. Whether or not Absalon himself drew up the Canute ritual, he must have had considerable knowledge of the most advanced practice in ecclesiastical music. He had studied in Paris as one of the first of a long succession of Scandinavian students during the twelfth and thirteenth centuries, the period when the Notre Dame school of composition flourished, and also when the sequence came into full bloom under the care of Adam of the Abbey of St. Victor. Scandinavian scholars were so numerous in Paris that by the end of the thirteenth century they had their own *collegium danicum* and *domus Daciae*; Danes may have been in a majority, but there were also Norwegians, Swedes, and Icelanders.

The most interesting Norwegian compositions that survive from the thirteenth century are the Magnus-hymn and another hymn contained in the same manuscript;[2] this begins *Ex te oritus, O dulcis Scotus*, and alludes to the marriage of King Erik Magnusson to Margaret, daughter of Alexander III of Scotland at Bergen in 1281.[3] There are also two sequences connected with the cult of St. Olav at Nidaros; they begin *Lux illuxit letabunda* and *Predicasti Dei care* and were discovered at the beginning of the present century in the parchment wrappings of sixteenth-century account books.[4]

[1] *Codex Kiloniensis* (S.H./84/8vo).

[2] *Codex Upsaliensis* (C 233).

[3] Beveridge, John, 'Two Scottish Thirteenth Century Songs' in *Music and Letters*, Oct. 1939 (Vol. XX). Facsimiles of both hymns are given.

[4] Reiss, Georg, *Norske middelalderlige Musikhaandskrifter*, Christiania, 1908; *Musiken ved den middelalderlige Olavsdyrkelse i Norden*, Christiania, 1912. See Plate V.

A full account of music in Trondheim Cathedral in the thirteenth

The wealth of the mediaeval Swedish hymns and sequences has been revealed by the studies of Professor Carl-Allan Moberg.[1] The influence of British missionaries on the earlier phases of the church in Sweden was extensive; for example, a leaf from a hymnary or kalendar of the early twelfth century, perhaps used in the diocese of Linköping, mentions not only the Danish St. Canute and the Norwegian St. Olav, but also the English St. Botolph. The earliest documents for the Swedish hymns date from the first part of the thirteenth century, and show that a parody-technique was widely used, new verses being composed to older metrical schemes and fitted to plainsong melodies. Among the saints commemorated in this way were St. Erik, martyred in 1138 during a crusade led by the English-born Bishop Henry of Uppsala against the pagan Finns; St. Eskil, another British monk martyred by the Svear in the latter part of the eleventh century; and St. David, also from Britain. The verses on St. Henry contained in a sequence in an early printed *graduale suecanum* from about 1500 refer to his English birth and to the manner of his death:

> *Ortus in Britannia,*
> *pollens Dei gracia,*
> *superna providencia*
> *pontifex efficitur*
> *clarus in Upsalia.*
> *Demum pro iusticia*
> *decertans in Finlandia*
> *pugil Christi moritur.*

('Born in Britain, strong in divine grace, by almighty providence became the renowned Bishop of Uppsala. At length, fighting for righteousness in Finland, he died a warrior of Christ.')

A sequence on St. Erik occurs in another Swedish manuscript[2]

century is given by Oluf Kolsrud in 'Korsongen i Nidarosdomen', contributed to *Festskrift til O. M. Sandvik*, Oslo, 1945.

[1] Moberg, Carl-Allan, *Über die Schwedischen Sequenzen*, Uppsala, 1927; *Die liturgischen Hymnen in Schweden*, Copenhagen, 1947. See also Moberg's article *Sveriges, Norges och Danmarks Kyrkomusik* and Haapanen, T.: *Kyrkomusiken i Finland under Medeltiden*, both in *Nordisk Kultur*.

[2] *Codex Upsaliensis* (C 513). See Plate IIIb.

which may have been written in England or in Sweden under English influence. The Erik sequence, *Gratulemur dulci prosa*, is set to a melody that has not been traced to any foreign source. By the end of the fifteenth century a special feast commemorated the patron saints of the Swedish church—Erik, Henry, Eskil, Botvid, David, Sigfrid, Helen and Birgitta, and a sequence beginning *Exsultant angelorum chori* mentions them all by name. St. Birgitta (1303–1373) holds a special place in hymnology. One of the most dynamic and versatile figures of the Middle Ages, she founded a double convent at Vadstena and inspired the compilation of a series of hymns for the use of her Order in their seven daily services.[1]

St. Birgitta's austere rule forbade the use of polyphony at Vadstena, but the practice of *organum* singing in the Paris style was encouraged in the cathedral at Uppsala much earlier than her time. Unfortunately the libraries of Uppsala and Vadstena were both destroyed or dispersed during the Reformation period; the former contained about a hundred volumes in 1369, and the Vadstena collection, probably the finest in Sweden, had 1,400 books, a few of which found their way into the university library as a gift from Gustavus Adolphus. Many manuscripts, including musical texts, were cut up to make bindings for account books, tax schedules and other prosaic documents, or were used by soldiers as wadding for their muskets in the wars of the sixteenth century. About 50,000 parchment leaves have survived in bindings, and further evidence of the widespread use of liturgical books in mediaeval Sweden is provided by the Laws of Småland (about 1300), where the minimum parish library is enumerated as a massbook, an antiphonal, a psalter, and a gradual.

During the last few years of the fifteenth century and at the beginning of the sixteenth, on the eve of the Reformation, printed liturgical books were purchased in considerable numbers for use in Danish, Swedish and Norwegian dioceses. By this time the cathedral churches had large and efficient choirs, judging by the material imported from Flanders and other

---

[1] Most of these compositions are attributed to Petrus Olavi, St. Birgitta's confessor. They were translated into Swedish in 1510 by 'Käre fadhe confessor generalis her nigils rauldi'. See Svanfeldt, N., *Sång och Visbok*, Stockholm, 1936.

musically advanced regions for their use. An ordinance of Christian II of Denmark provided for the maintenance of choral services in all cathedrals, and for schoolmasters to rehearse their choristers in *den ny Mensure*, in order that they might sing High Mass in mensural settings at all festivals. In contrast to this evidence of elaborate church music in southern Scandinavia is a curious survival of more primitive part-singing, recorded in the remains of a choir-book written out in 1473 in the Benedictine monastery of Munke-Tväraa, in northern Iceland.[1] The contents include fragments of an *Agnus Dei* and a *Credo* with an upper part added to the plainsong, making note against note counterpoint chiefly in fifths and octaves with occasional thirds, and with much crossing of parts.

The earliest known notation of a secular song in Scandinavia is found at the end of the late thirteenth century portion of a manuscript known as *Codex runicus*,[2] and containing the Laws of Skåne and other memoranda, all written in runic characters. The melody is written in square notation on two four-lined staves with a C clef; and at the end of the second stave stands what looks at first sight like a complicated ligature. The accompanying text, in runes, gives the first two lines of a ballad:

Drømdae mik aen drøm inat
um silki ok aerlik pael.

('I dreamed a dream last night of silk and fine attire.')
The remaining two lines that would complete the ballad-stanza are missing, and there is no refrain. The scribe no doubt abandoned the attempt to write the complete stanza in the restricted space left on the page, and only just crowded in the second half of the melody by using a ligature-like scrawl as a shorthand device. Angul Hammerich[3] reconstructed the whole melody, with a conjectural refrain or *omkvaed* (see page 29). The first strain has been adopted as an interval signal by the Danish State Radio.

Although there are no other known examples of both words and tune of a ballad having been written down in mediaeval Scandinavia, there is abundant testimony from literary sources

[1] Now in the Arnamagnaean Collection, Copenhagen (AM 8vo 80).
[2] AM 8vo 28. See Plate IV.
[3] Hammerich, Angul, *Dansk Musikhistorie*, Copenhagen, 1921, pp. 79 seq.

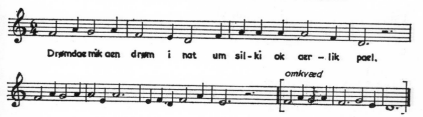

Drømdoe mik aen drøm i nat um sil-ki ok aer-lik poel.

omkvæd

that the ballad enjoyed a long spell of popularity, beginning—probably under French influence—in the Middle Ages and continuing into modern times. It still endures as a living tradition in the Faeroe Islands, where the chanting of ballads (*kvaedir*) is combined, as it was in the Middle Ages, with a species of chain dance, apparently derived from the *carole* and consisting of two steps to the left and one to the right, with the song and dance leader at the head of the chain.[1] A dance of this kind is depicted in a fresco dating from about 1380 in Ørslev church in Zealand. While the stanzas were, and still are in the Faeroes, often improvised, and the stanza melodies freely adapted and interchanged from song to song, the choral refrain or *omkvaed* is invariable, being built out of melodic formulae that are doubtless of great antiquity. The usual rhythmic pattern of the stanza is made up of four lines with four and three stresses alternately; the second and fourth lines generally rhyme, and the second half of the stanza may be sung to the same melodic phrase as the first. The *omkvaed* is metrically of variable length; melodically it forms a coda, sometimes derived from the initial phrase of the stanza melody. The subject matter may be mythological, or it may deal with historical events and persons, like the song about Canute the Great's daughter Gunhild, which William of Malmesbury mentions as being sung in the streets of his own time (about 1140).[2] The following is an example of the Danish historical ballad, relating the story of the murder of King Erik Klipping in 1286, and probably composed soon afterwards. The verses are found in sixteenth-century manuscript collections; the tune was taken down from peasant singing by the collector, E. Tang Kristensen in 1869 (see Plate XIX), and revised by Thomas Laub:

[1] Thuren, Hjalmar, *Folkesangen paa Faeroerne*, Copenhagen, 1908.
[2] Quoted in Entwistle, W. J., *European Balladry*, Oxford, 1939, p. 67.

29

('There are so many in Denmark, who would all be master; they rode to Ribe and had clothes made for them (*refrain*). Now stands the country in danger.' [Disguised as monks, the conspirators ambush the King as he sets out for Finderup; they kill him, and a page carries the news to Erik's queen.]

Interesting examples of the legendary ballad are the story of Siegfried, still sung as *Sjúrdar kvaedi* in the Faeroes;[1] and *Valravnen*, recorded with its tune in Corvinus' *Heptachordum Danicum* in 1646—one of the earliest attempts to reproduce a popular tune in an academic treatise. According to Corvinus, it was the custom to sing the *omkvaed* at the beginning of the Valravnen ballad as well as at the end of each stanza.[2]

[1] The melody of this ballad was the first Fareoese tune to be printed. It was taken down by A. F. Winding from a Fareoese singer, Povl Johnsen, in 1818 and published as an appendix to Lyngbye's *Faerøiske Qvaeder*.

[2] Rhythm and barring from Abrahamson, Nyerup and Rahbek, *Udvalgte danske Viser fra Middelalderen*. Valravnen is a monster with some of the

('The monster flies in the evening, he cannot fly by day; he shall have ill-fortune, good luck he cannot gain. (*refrain*) But the monster flies in the evening.')

The compilation of manuscript books of ballad-verses was a fashionable courtly pursuit in the sixteenth century; a curious example is the 'heart-book' written about 1553–5 by Albert Muus, head cook of the royal household.[1] The first printed collection of the words of a number of ballads, edited by Anders Sørensen Vedel in 1591 and republished by Peder Syv in 1695, was to have a wide circulation among all classes, not only in Denmark but also in Norway and the Faeroes. But only exceptionally were melodies recorded at this period, one of the exceptions being the tune of *Oluf Strangesøn* which Vedel himself jotted down about 1580 above the words of the ballad in the so-called Rentzel's MS.[2] His version tallies closely with the melody to the same ballad noted by Lindeman in Sauland, Norway, in 1860, and with a phonograph recording made in the Faeroes in 1929.[3]

Though the ballad became closely interwoven with the traditional lore of the Scandinavian peasantry, and embodied so much national legend and history, it was not an entirely indigenous literary or musical form. On the contrary, it was of courtly origin and seems to have reached the North during the thirteenth century, at a time when a number of celebrated poets and singers were visitors to the Scandinavian courts. Several of the German Minnesinger are known to have been guests of the Danish kings, and to have repaid hospitality with songs in praise of their royal hosts. Reimar von Zweter made laudatory

characteristics of the werewolf. For a comparison between Corvinus' version and a variant recorded in recent times in the Faeroes, see the article 'Folksong (Denmark)' in *Grove's Dictionary* (5th edtn.).

Apart from the tune actually quoted, Corvinus' chapter on taking down a tune from oral tradition ('Melodiam quamcunque ab illiteratis aliisve inventam, systemati musico inscribere') is an interesting summary of collectors' methods throughout the centuries: 'Exempli gratiâ, si quis audiret cani aliquam è cantilenis nostratibus tam Ecclesiasticis quam profanis, quas vulgô *Gigantum* nominamus, quam nunquam antea audivisset, quomodo tamen è sono percepto Melodiam certis iisq; debitis Notis exciperet atq; effingeret', etc. (p. 92, original edtn.).

[1] See Plate XIV.
[2] Gl. Kgl. S. 2397, 4to.
[3] Grüner Nielsen, H., *Folkemusik i Danmark*, in *Nordisk Kultur XXV*.

verses on King Erik Ploughpenny, Tannhäuser and Rumelant on King Erik Klipping, and Frauenlob on King Erik Menvet. Rumelant describes the death of Erik Klipping, which as we have seen was made the subject of a Danish ballad:

> *Tzu ivtland in dem nordhen*
> *dar ist begangen mortlich mort,*
> *si kvnden iren kvninc vnsanfte wecken*
> *Of eynen bette da her slief.*
> *Sex vnd vivnftich wunden tief*
> *Durchstachen ym die recken.*

('In Jutland in the north a wicked murder has been done. They roughly awakened their King from a bed where he slept. The warriors stabbed him with six and fifty deep wounds.')[1]

The Minnesinger, or their minstrels, may well have introduced new instruments, particularly those played with the bow, into the northern countries.[2] Although one of the usual Norse terms for a stringed instrument, *gigja*, occurs as far back as the tenth century as a personal name in Iceland, and although this word is found side by side with another term, *fidla*, implying that they are distinct instruments, it is not certain that either denoted a bowed instrument until the twelfth or thirteenth century. Even in the ballads, where *fidla*, *fiol*, and *viol* are the usual terms, the word *harpa* and its cognates are occasionally used as synonyms. By the fifteenth century, however, bowed viols are represented in mural paintings in Danish and Swedish churches, together with other Renaissance instruments, like the lute, organistrum, psaltery, bells, and large triangles at Häverö, and the bagpipes painted on a Finnish church roof by the late fifteenth-century artist Petrus Henriksson.

---

[1] Hammerich, A., *Dansk Musikhistorie*, pp. 72 seq.
[2] For a full discussion of these instruments, see Panum, op. cit., and Andersson, Otto, *The Bowed Harp*, London, 1930.

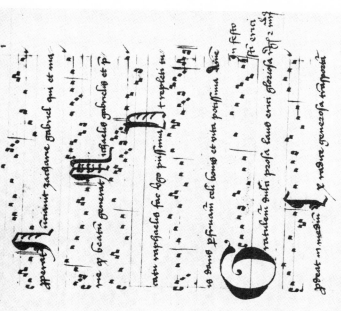

IIIb *Gratulemur dulci prosa*: opening of sequence for Festival of St. Erik, possibly by Jakob Israelson, Archbishop of Uppsala (d. 1281); *from Codex upsaliensis* (C513)

Reproduced by courtesy of Uppsala University Library and The Swedish Institute, London

IIIa *Concordemus in hac die*: opening of sequence attributed to Archbishop Birger Gregerson, fourteenth century; *from Codex upsaliensis* (C513)

IV Page from facsimile of *Codex runicus* (ca. 1296–1319) showing notation of part of Danish ballad; original in Arnamagnaean Collection (AM 8vo 28)

2

The Reformation: Music in Church, School and Court

The spread of the Lutheran reformed church to Scandinavia during the early decades of the sixteenth century helped to strengthen cultural and political ties with northern Germany, and led to fruitful developments in literature and music.

In Denmark and Norway the Reformation began under the reigns of Frederik I (1523–33) and Christian II (1533–36), and was completed by the Articles of Ribe in 1542 under Christian III (1536–59). Following the printing of the Bible in the Danish language in 1550, a series of psalm and service books appeared. One of the most influential was Hans Thomissøn's *Den danske Psalmebog*, published in 1569 and containing 268 metrical psalms, of which 150 were in Danish and the rest in German; the tunes were mostly taken from among those already in use in Lutheran Germany. Thomissøn's psalter was adopted throughout Denmark and Norway, copies being chained to the reading-desks of parish churches. It was supplemented in 1573 by Niels Jesperssøn's gradual, a finely printed volume published by order of Frederik II (1559–88), which retained some of the Latin office hymns along with Danish adaptations. A complete psalter was provided by Anders Arreboe's *Kong Davids Psalter sangviiz udsat* (1623, melody edition four years later). Iceland had its own chorale book (*grallari*) by 1594, and retained it unchanged through nineteen editions until 1779; an appendix to the sixth edition gives directions for singing from notes, drawn up by Bishop Gudbrandir Thorláksson.

With Sweden the process of church reforms was less peaceful. Its first stirrings were felt among the German colony in Stockholm; religious questions soon became complicated by political issues, and a crisis occurred after the massacre of Stockholm in 1520, when the nationalist party, supported by the peasants of Dalecarlia and led by the young nobleman Gustav Eriksson Vasa, defeated the army of Christian II, thus ending the Union of Kalmar that had held Denmark, Norway and Sweden precariously together since 1397. The story of Gustav Vasa and the Dalecarlians was cherished in popular memory and became the theme of a ballad, *Konung Gösta rider till Dalarna*.

After his election as King of Sweden in 1523, Gustav made Stockholm the royal capital instead of Uppsala, expelled the Catholic Archbishop, and gave the heads of the Lutheran church, Olaus Petri and his brother Laurentius, important offices of state. Laurentius also became the first Protestant Archbishop of Uppsala. The new government imposed protective tariffs and, like the Protestant government in Denmark, confiscated church property, including conventual and cathedral libraries. Liturgical reform followed much the same course as in other Lutheran countries; the sermon was given greater prominence, the whole Bible was made available in 1541 in the Swedish language, and the Epistle and Gospel were ordered to be read in the native tongue. Olaus Petri made translations and paraphrases of Latin and German hymns that still form the backbone of the Swedish chorale book, and the new hymnody quickly spread to town and country parishes, where the parish clerks became the principal agents in teaching and leading congregational singing. The King himself was opposed, however, to a complete abandonment of the Catholic liturgy, and the *Articuli ordinantiae* of 1540 permitted an elaborate ritual in the larger churches on high festivals, including the use of organs and polyphonic choral settings. Latin continued to be used in the Swedish mass far into the sixteenth century; a council of bishops held at Uppsala in 1583 ordained that a Latin mass should be sung on high festivals in churches where a reasonable proportion of the congregation might be expected to follow it, while Swedish mass was being celebrated at a side altar.

Gustav Vasa had had the liberal education of a Renaissance nobleman and played the lute; his successors on the Swedish throne showed even stronger musical interests. Gustav's first son, Erik XIV (1560–68), attempted polyphonic composition,[1] and Johan III (1568–92) instituted elaborate services in the royal chapel and collected material for the choir from the works of such composers as Lassus, Giovanni Gabriel Hassler, Isaac, and Senfl. The royal choir was by no means the only one in Sweden that could perform difficult contrapuntal music; from the contents of choir-school libraries it is clear that large and ambitious choirs existed at this time in other centres, such as Enköping, Kalmar, Växjö, and Strangnäs. These choir-schools had been established by Laurentius Petri to take the place of the old monastic schools.[2]

One of the choir-schools, at Åbo in Finland,[3] deserves special mention as the place where Didrik (or Theodoric) Peter of Nyland began to compile his famous collection of songs known as *Piae Cantiones*. Didrik left the choir-school in 1580 to study at Åbo University, and his book, completed while he was still a student, was published in 1582 at Greifswald, near Rostock, which was then in Swedish territory. *Piae Cantiones ecclesiasticae et scholasticae* is believed to be the earliest Swedish musical work to be printed in mensural notation. A Finnish version, without tunes, was published in Stockholm in 1616, a second edition of the tune book appeared at Rostock in 1625, and there were several subsequent reprints. Many of the songs remained popular in Sweden and Finland throughout the nineteenth century, and since then have gained a far wider circulation through the English translations of Neale, Woodward and others.[4]

The original collection contained fifty-two songs, but later editions increased this number to nearly eighty. All have rhyming Latin texts, with a few alternative Swedish versions. Most of the settings are monodic; some have been traced to German or French sources, but others, like the splendid tune to

[1] Part of a vocal work in eight parts, attributed to Erik XIV, is reproduced in Norlind, T., *Från Tyska Kyrkans Glansdagar*, I, p. 19, Stockholm, 1944–5.

[2] For a comprehensive study of this and other aspects of Swedish music from the Reformation period to the end of the seventeenth century, see Moberg, C.-A., *Från kyrko- och hovmusik till offentlig konsert*, Uppsala, 1942.

[3] Finland became a Swedish grand duchy in 1582.

[4] *Piae Cantiones* was reprinted in 1910 by the Plainsong and Mediaeval Music Society (edtd. Rev. G. R. Woodward).

Personent hodie, seem to be of Swedish or Finnish origin, and may be taken from secular folksong. There are also about a dozen settings in simple polyphony for two, three or four voices, including two examples of *Stimmtausch,* or interchange of voices, in the two-part *Ad cantus laetitiae* and *Zachaeus arboris ascendit stipitem*—the latter quaintly pictorial in its suggestion of Zacchaeus climbing the tree and looking down.

The scholastic intentions of *Piae cantiones* is evident not only in the simplicity of the settings, which are admirably suited to treble and immature adult male voices, but also in the texts with their many references to school life: *Psallat scholarum concio, O scholares discite, O scholares voce pares, Laetemur omnes socii,* and *Scholares convenite* which pokes fun at inept choristers who are ignorant of musical theory and grammar ('*Vix sciunt G, Ut, A, Re, nec Musa declinare*'). Several songs allude to the changing seasons of the year: *In hoc anni circulo, Cedit hyems eminus,* and *Tempus adest floridum,* the spring song that Neale unfortunately robbed of its attractive tune for his own carol *Good King Wenceslas.* Another fine spring carol, *In vernalis temporis ortu laetabundo,* has a text of Danish origin, attributed to Morten Börup, rector of the Latin school at Aarhus at the beginning of the sixteenth century. Peter of Nyland may have learnt these verses, and perhaps the tune also, from his Danish grandfather who had been a pupil in Börup's school.

('At the happy beginning of springtime, when the swallow

36

V *Lux illuxit letabunda*: opening of sequence for Festival of St. Olav; from
  Riksarkivet (National Archives of Norway) (R 986 b)

VIa & b Wind music from the Court of Christian III of Denmark; Royal
Library, Copenhagen (4to 1872 and 1873)

brings tidings of the cold's retreat, the beauty of land, sea, and woods is seen out of doors as the world renews itself. Bodily vigour returns, grief of heart disappears, at this joyful time.')

Another Scandinavian feature is the inclusion of songs celebrating native saints in acrostic verses; St. Olaf, for example, is commemorated in a song beginning 'Olla mortis patescit'. But the variety and perennial freshness of *Piae Cantiones* have long been a gift from Scandinavia to the whole Christian world, as reference to the indexes of almost any modern book of hymns or carols will show.

Choir-schools flourished in Denmark also, and the texts of some of their schoolboy plays have come down to us with the original music. One deals with the life and death of St. Canute Lavard; the rhymed text is mostly in Danish, and introduces a song for the messenger from Earl Magnus, who has been ordered to entice Canute into the wood of Haraldsted to be murdered. According to Saxo Grammaticus, the messenger was a Saxon singer who took pity on his victim and tried to warn him by singing the traditional ballad of Grimhild's betrayal and murder of his brother; but the playwright turns the singer into a Dane and introduces his warning song with the rubric: 'Tyrne Hette nuncians ducem de insidiis Magni his verbis et cantat'. Three more plays survive from a series by Hieronymus Justessøn Ranch (1539–1607), a canon of Viborg. One of them entitled *Samsons Faegsel* ('Samson's Captivity') introduces nine songs whose tunes, though not recorded in notation, can be identified as borrowings from popular songs of the day, such as the German *Venus du und dein Kind* which Dalila's attendants sing at their spinning-wheels. To Ranch is also attributed a delightful *Fuglevise* ('Bird-song'), which may well have been written for school use: the verses first appear in print in 1617, the tune in 1630. Various wild birds are named and described, and the song ends with a moralizing stanza. The melody has a spontaneous and fresh simplicity. (See page 38.)

The growing wealth and prestige of the Scandinavian kingdoms was reflected in the growth of court ceremonial and its appropriate music. The Danish royal trumpeter-corps, which included sackbut and kettledrum players and exponents of other wind instruments such as the krumhorn and zinck, could

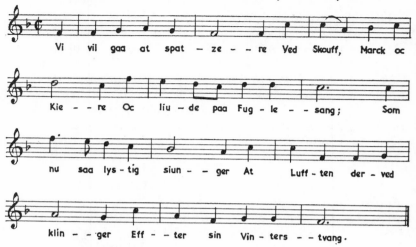

('We will go and walk by wood, field and pool and listen to the song of the birds. Their singing is so cheerful that all the air rings with it, after the harshness of winter.')[1]

---

trace its privileges back to the beginning of the Oldenburg dynasty and the fanfares sounded on the accession of Christian I in 1448. Some of the fraternity enjoyed international fame, being excellent all-round musicians like Jørgen Heyde, who served first at the court of Count Albrecht of Prussia, then from 1542 to 1556 as chief trumpeter to Christian III of Denmark, afterwards held an appointment under Count John of Finland, and finally became head of the Swedish court band with sixteen instrumentalists at his disposal, including six Italian string players.

Two sets of part books in the Royal Library at Copenhagen[2] throw light on the repertory of the musicians at Christian III's court, and show how they attempted to provide for the musical requirements of both chapel and banqueting hall. The earlier set, bearing on their stamped leather covers the date 1541, consists of seven part-books filled with sacred and secular compositions, ranging from vocal works in four to nine parts to dances and other instrumental pieces for entertainment. The

[1] Complete Danish text in *Gamle Danske Viser*, edtd. A. Arnholtz, N. Schiørring, and F. Viderø, Hefte 2, Copenhagen, 1942.

[2] *Gl. Kgl. Saml.*, 4to, 1872 and 1873.

church composers represented include directors of the Danish chapel in Christian III's time—Mattz Hack, David Ebell, Adrian Peter Coclicus, and Jørgen (or Georgius) Preston who may have been of English origin. There are also pieces by the Netherlanders Verdelot, Brumel, Josquin, Fevin, Gombert, Mouton, and Willaert; by the Germans Senfl and Finck; and by the Italian Festa. Some of the instrumental pieces are for specific wind ensembles, including trombone and cromorne ('auf pusaun und krumhorn'), cornetts and trombones (*Laudate Dominum mit 8 Stimmen auf 4 Zincken und 4 Pusaunen*), and cromorne consort (*D'Andernach auff dem Reine, auf Krumbhörner*). There is also[1] a piece of programme music on the Battle of Pavia (*Die Schlacht paffia*), full of brass fanfares. The later set of part-books lacks the alto, but the remaining five books are highly interesting, and are notably elegant in writing and binding. The covers are dated 1556. The discant book bears the name of Erhart Herdegen, who succeeded Heyde as chief trumpeter and was entrusted with the teaching of several pupils on trumpet, zinck and other instruments. Some of the contents of these later books illustrate the style of ceremonial trumpet-playing practised at the Danish court (see Plate VIb). A rhymed account of music at the coronation and wedding of Christian III's successor, Frederik II (1559–1588) fills in the picture, although the writer may have drawn upon his experience of court music at a somewhat later date (1574) when the verses appeared in print:

> Man maatte of høre der lystige Spil,
> mens Maaltidet vared, jeg sige og vil,
> med Zitara, Tromper, med Harper og Gie,
> med kunstige og herlige Zimfonie,
> Basuner og Sincker og Positiv,
> Skalmeier, Trometer og Kromhorn stiv. . . .
> Den ene lod af, den anden gegynde.
> De Sangere sig og stundom fremskynde,
> de sjunge mest et Stykke saa fin.
> frantzosk, italisk og saa latin
> med danske og tyske jeg siger for sand.[2]

[1] See Plate VIa.

[2] Quoted in Ravn, V. C., *Konserter og musikalske Selskaber i aeldre Tid*, Copenhagen, 1886.

('There one might hear cheerful music throughout the meal, I will assert, with lutes(?), trumscheits(?), with harps and fiddles, with skilful and fine consort, trombones and cornetts and positive organ, shawms, trumpets, and bold krummhorn. . . . As one left off another began. The singers joined in from time to time; they sang many a rare piece, in French, Italian and Latin too, as well as Danish and German—I tell the truth.')

Frederik II enlarged the royal band, not only maintaining the trumpeter-corps but also adding a body of strings (*giglere*). This was the origin of *Det kongelige Kapel*, a name which at first denoted the whole musical establishment of choir and orchestra, but now survives as the honourable designation of a purely orchestral body. Frederik II summoned David Abell (or Ebell) from Lübeck, at that time the nearest great musical centre near Denmark, to take charge of the court music. The chapel part-books contain several compositions by Abell, including a six-part setting of *In dulci jubilo*.[1] Otherwise most of the composers mentioned in connection with the *Cantori* or royal choir at this period appear to have been Netherlanders; the most distinguished of them was Adrian Petit Coclicus, who came from Nüremberg, where he had published his four-part psalms and his *Compendium musices*, and settled in Denmark for the last years of his life—from 1556 to 1562—in the service of Christian III and Frederik II. The royal part-books contain two five-part works and a motet in eight parts, *Si consurrexistis*, by this talented, vigorous and often unruly personage whose portrait in woodcut enlivens the solid learning of his *Compendium musices*.[2]

The cultural life of the Danish court reached its zenith during the long reign of Christian IV (1588–1648), a striking figure in Danish history and one of the most magnificent of the late Renaissance princes. His court was open to all men of distinction in the arts or literature, whatever their country, but above all Christian encouraged architects and musicians. He was himself a competent amateur performer, and liked to have his court band with him on his journeys about the realm. His patronage was sought, and obtained, by composers of the

[1] Reprinted in the series *Dansk Mensural-Cantori*, Nr. 7, Skandinavisk Musikforlag, Copenhagen, 1946.

[2] Facsimile reprint in *Documenta musicologica*, Bd. 9, Bärenreiter-Verlag.

quality of Michael Praetorius and Orazio Vecchi, both of whom dedicated works to him. Christian's love of architecture is even better known. In Copenhagen he largely determined the unique character of the old town with buildings such as Rosenborg Castle, the Stock Exchange with its fantastic spire, the Round Tower, the Arsenal, and the Docks; and at Hillerød, north of the capital, he built the huge Renaissance palace of Frederiksborg, in the chapel of which the Compenius chamber organ, completed a few years earlier, was installed in 1617. This beautifully-fashioned instrument is kept tuned to the untempered scale, and is regularly used for recitals; it has two manuals and a pedal clavier, the latter controlling as many stops as there are on each of the manuals.[1]

Carillons were introduced into Denmark at this period; the Frederiksborg palace acquired one in 1620, made in Nordhausen in the Harz mountains, and towards the end of his reign Christian IV presented a chime of nineteen bells to the Church of the Holy Spirit in Copenhagen. Both of these carillons were destroyed by fire, the former when part of the palace was burnt down in 1859 (at which time the Compenius organ was fortunately being housed elsewhere), and the Holy Spirit carillon, still playing the chorale *Wend' ab deinen Zorn lieber Gott mit Gnaden*, in the conflagration that swept the capital in 1728.

As the brother-in-law of James I of England, Christian IV encouraged the interchange of musicians and actors between Denmark and England, whose excellence in both arts was everywhere acknowledged. As early as 1579 a company of

---

[1] The specification of the organ is as follows:

Upper manual		Lower manual		Pedal	
Principal	8	Quintadena	8	Subbas	16
Gedackt	8	Gedacktflöte	4	Gemshorn	8
Kleinprincipal	4	Principal Diskant	4	Quintadena	8
Gemshorn	4	Blockflöte Diskant	4	Querflöte	4
Nachthorn	4	Gemshorn	2	Nachthorn	2
Blockflöte	4	Nasat	1⅓	Bauerflöte	1
Gedacktquint	2⅔	Zimbell	⅛	Sordun	16
Gedacktflöte	2	Krumhorn	8	Dolcian	8
Rankett	16	Geigenregal	4	Regal	4

Accessories include two tremulants, two drone bass devices—one giving a bagpipe effect on F and C through three octaves—and a manual coupler. See Plate VII.

English *instrumentister* came to Frederik II's court and stayed there eight years, and in the year of their departure (1586) 'Wilhelm Kempe, instrumentist' together with other English 'instrumentister och springere' (i.e. dancers)[1] arrived at the royal castle of Helsingør—Shakespeare's Elsinore; it is not impossible that the future author of *Hamlet* may have been among the 'instrumentister', but in any event he would have been able to gather all the local colour he needed from his fellow-players in the Lord Chamberlain's company ten years later, since they included Will Kemp (surely an *instrumentist* by virtue of his skill on pipe and tabor), Bryan and Pope. They may have told Shakespeare about the custom of toast-drinking at the court of Christian IV while 'the kettledrum and trumpet . . . bray out The triumph of his pledge', a custom no less severely rebuked in *Hamlet* than it was to be half a century later, when the puritan Whitelocke encountered it at the Swedish court.

Our greatest song-composer and lutenist, John Dowland, certainly knew Elsinore. He served as lutenist to the Danish king from 1598 to 1606, being rewarded with the magnificent salary of five hundred *dalers* a year besides presents of money and jewellery. The title page of Dowland's *Second Book of Ayres* describes the composer as lutenist to the King of Denmark, and has a dedication addressed to Lady Lucie Countess of Bedford 'from Helsingnoure in Denmarke the first of June' (1600); the *Third Book of Ayres* published in 1603 carries a similar description of the composer's appointment with 'the most high and mightie Christian the fourth by the grace of God King of Denmark and Norway' etc., and in his epistle to the reader Dowland writes feelingly of the long sea-voyage between the two countries: 'My first two bookes of aires speed so well that they have produced a third, which they have fecht far from home, and brought even through the most perilous seas, where having escapt so many sharpe rocks, I hope they shall not be wrackt on land by curious and biting censures'. Dowland's *Lachrimae*, published in 1605 while he was still in Denmark, is inscribed to 'the most Gracious and Sacred Princess Anne, Queen of England, Scotland, France and Ireland', for by her marriage to James VI of Scotland the sister of Christian IV had

---

[1] Their names are given as George Bryan, Thomas Pope, Thomas Stevens, Thomas Koning (King), and Robert Persj (Percy).

united three royal houses. Although Dowland was finally dismissed from Christian's service for alleged financial misconduct his supreme artistry was remembered with reverence, and his son Robert seems to have found a place in the Danish court; he included in his *Varietie of Lute Lessons* (1610) a galliard 'commonly known by the name of the most high and mightie Christianus the fourth King of Denmarke, his Galliard'.

Not content with the Dowlands, Christian IV did his utmost to entice other English musicians to his court, sending John Dowland over to England in 1602 to buy instruments and enlist performers. Among English musicians known to have spent longer or shorter periods at Elsinore or Copenhagen are Thomas Robinson, who claims in the dedication of his *Schoole of Musicke* to James I that he has been lute-master to Princess Anne of Denmark; Daniel Norcombe, viol player and madrigalist; John Meinert (Maynard) the singer; William Brade and his son Christian; Thomas Cutting, lutenist and outstanding composer for his instrument; and Thomas Simpson, whose *Taffelconsort*, containing works by John Dowland and other Englishmen, appeared in Hamburg in 1621. An earlier collection published in 1607, also in Hamburg, and entitled *Auszerlesener Paduanen und Galliarden*, includes compositions by various musicians connected with the court of Christian IV, among them John Dowland and William Brade.[1]

Christian IV continued his predecessors' policy of employing foreign directors of court music: three served in succession during his reign—Gregorius Trehou, Melchior Borchgrevinck, and Heinrich Schütz—while Danes, Mogens Pederssøn, Hans Nielssøn, and Jacob Ørn, in turn occupied the post of deputy director. Borchgrevinck, whose strong bearded features may be discerned among the musicians in Cleyn's ceiling painting in the Knights' Hall of Rosenborg Castle,[2] was especially favoured by Christian IV, who sent him to Dantzig and London in search of instruments and singers, and in 1599 dispatched him with

---

[1] Examples of English instrumental works of the period are reprinted in score in 'Jacobean Consort Music' (*Musica Britannica*, Vol. IX, edtd. William Coates and Thurston Dart), London, 1955. See also Dart, T., 'Jacobean Consort Music' in *Proceedings of the Royal Musical Association*, 1954–5.

[2] See Plate VIII.

four other young men to study under Giovanni Gabrieli in Venice. On his return a year later, Borchgrevinck was made court organist and took charge of the further studies of two of his companions on the Italian journey, Hans Nielsen and Mogens Pedersøn. He became assistant to Gregorius Trehou and succeeded him as director of the court music in 1628. Borchgrevinck's compositions have fared unluckily; only six of the part-books containing an eight-part mass attributed to him have been preserved, and not a single copy of his psalm-settings, published in Copenhagen in 1607 under the title *IX Davids Psalmer med fire Stemmer* (in four parts) have survived. His two volumes of collected madrigals are, however, extant; they were published in Copenhagen under the title *Giardino novo bellissimo di varii fiori musicali sceltissimi*, the first volume being dedicated to Christian IV in 1605 and the second to James I of England in the following year. The contents are drawn from the works of Flemish and Italian masters, including Monteverdi, and from a few Danish contemporaries, including Hans Nielsen, who under his assumed Italian name of Giovanni Fonteijo had published two books of his own five-part madrigals in Venice in 1606.

The most distinguished native Danish composer of the early baroque period was Mogens Pedersøn, who was born in 1585, travelled to Venice first with Borchgrevinck as already stated, and again in 1608 to spend four more years as pupil of Giovanni Gabrieli. His first book of Italian madrigals, dedicated to Christian IV, was published in Venice in 1608; his other unpublished work, *Pratum spirituale*, appeared in Copenhagen in 1620. After a three-year visit to England, from 1611 to 1614, in company with two other Danes, Jacob Ørn and Hans Brachrogg, he returned to the Danish court to assist in the direction of what was at that time one of the largest musical establishments in Europe, comprising thirty-one singers and thirty instrumentalists, beside the sixteen court trumpeters.

In his Italian madrigals Pedersøn uses the structural and colouristic devices perfected by Marenzio. There is humour in the word-painting of *Lascia, semplice* where the white-haired lover compares himself to an old log quickly consumed by a small flame, while the green branch of his rival's affection burns reluctantly; and the two parts of *Madonn' Amor ed io can-*

VII Compenius Organ in the chapel of Frederiksborg Castle, Hillerod.
The pedal clavier is folded into the lower part of the case when not in use

VIII Groups of musicians from ceiling painting by Franz Cleyn (ca. 1620) in Rosenborg Palace, Copenhagen. The different groups are playing bowed strings, lutes, cornetti and sackbuts

tan' insiem' un giorno are an amusing fantasy on musical terms. The *Pratum spirituale* is described on the title-page as containing 'Masses, psalms and motets such as are used in Denmark and Norway', and is dedicated to Prince Christian (V), the seventeen-year-old heir-apparent, for whose education the composer had evidently been partly responsible. The contents of the *Pratum* are varied in scale and style. There are three Latin five-part motets, extended free compositions in the early

Reproduced by permission of Munksgaard A/S, Copenhagen.

('O Lord, save me and judge my cause against the evil host, and against the man bound in deceit and sore wickedness. For thou art all my strength and counsel; why doest thou let me go thus afflicted and oppressed by mine enemies?')

baroque manner, and obviously designed for the royal chapel. In contrast is a series of twenty-eight simple homophonic settings, mostly in five parts, of Danish metrical psalms, the tunes being chiefly from Hans Thomissøn's psalter and Niels Jesperssøn's gradual, which in turn are indebted to the German chorale books.[1] The example on page 45, however, is based on a chorale for which no German antecedent is known.

The *Pratum* also contains portions of both Latin and Danish masses, thus illustrating the tolerant attitude that obtained towards the liturgy in Denmark and Sweden. The Latin mass is written in free five-part contrapuntal style, and consists of *Kyrie, Gloria,* a shortened *Credo* and *Sanctus*—the customary abridgement of the Ordinary as used in Lutheran churches at this time. The Danish mass is quite different, being made up of chorale-like psalm-settings—a *kyrie*-psalm, a *gloria*-psalm, and a *credo*-psalm. There are three settings of the *kyrie* for use at special seasons, each based on a plainsong melody. The *gloria* is the Danish paraphrase *Aleneste Gud in Himmerig,* and the *credo* is a setting of its translation *Wi tro allesammen paa en Gud* with the plainsong in the tenor. Among the entirely original parts of the *Pratum* are sets of choral responses in both Latin and Danish; the final *Amen* from the latter is worth quoting:

[1] The complete works of Mogens Pedersøn have been reprinted as Vol. I of *Dania Sonans,* with an introduction by Knud Jeppesen, Copenhagen, 1933.

With the increased wealth and leisure enjoyed by middle and upper class society in the Baltic towns during the seventeenth century came a demand for collections of secular songs and instrumental pieces that amateurs could perform. One of the earliest secular song-books, printed at Sorø in 1642, was the work of Gabriel Voigtländer, a German who entered the service of Prince Christian (V) at Nykøbing castle in 1639 and described himself as 'Hoff-Feld Trommeter und Musicus'. The title of his collection indicates the wide scope of instrumental practice that must by now have been fairly common in the domestic circle: *Allehand Oden und Lieder, bey Clavicembalem Lauten Tiorben Pandora Violen di Gamba . . . zu gebrauchen.* The words of the songs are German, but it was not long before Danish verses, like the lines addressed by the poet-bishop Thomas Kingo to his wife Chrysallis, were adapted to the melodies of *Allehand Oden und Lieder,* which went through five editions between 1642 and 1664. Some of the *Oden* also appeared in translations in the first collection of Danish songs with melodies: this was the work of Søren Terkelsen, at one time an official at the court of Christian IV, and its title *Astree Sjungekor* was taken from a fashionable French romance.[1] The tunes were drawn from French, Dutch, English and German songs and instrumental works; and some of them were readapted to pietistic use in Kingo's *Aandelige Sjungekor* ('Spiritual choir') published in 1675. The example on page 48 from Terkelsen's collection is a translation from the German of Johann Rist. The *Daphnis* melody became extremely popular in both Germany and Denmark, and the whole song is typical of the pastoral convention that governed much secular song at this period.

The same period saw the publication of the first important theoretical work on music by a Danish author. We have already noticed in passing Hans Mikkelsen Ravn's interesting quotation of the melody and first stanza of the traditional ballad, *Raffnen hand flyffer om Afftenen.*[2] This occurs in *Heptachordum Danicum, seu nova solmisatio,* published in 1646 under Ravn's Latinized name

---

[1] *Astrée,* by Honoré d'Urfé, part of which Terkelsen had translated under the title of *Dend Hyrdinde Astrea.*

[2] See page 30.

('Daphnis went for some days over the green meadows and secretly began to lament his sorrow that was great and heavy. He sang from his burdened heart of the bitter pain of love: Alas that I may not see thee, O my fair Galathea.')

of Corvinus. The author, who also wrote on linguistic subjects,[1]

[1] *Ex rhythmologia danica*, Søro, 1649. Corvinus had a forerunner in this field, Peder Jensen Roskilde, whose *Prosodia danicae linguae* also contains experimental musical settings of rhythmic patterns, ascribed to Niels Haleg, former canon of Roskilde.

was one of a number of Danish and Swedish university men who cultivated musicological studies and also stimulated the practical performance of music in academic circles during the sixteenth and seventeenth centuries. Under the constitution of Copenhagen University in 1539 one of the lecturers was to be reader in music with responsibility for arranging performances of discant and figured music in the university church on festival days, and of encouraging the students to practise on 'organis, fistulis et fidibus' (organ, woodwind, and strings). The earliest occupant of the post, Mattz Hack, also lectured in mathematics and was one of the royal court composers.

The last and the greatest of the foreign musicians associated with Denmark under the reign of Christian IV was Heinrich Schütz, who was induced by Prince Christian (V) to leave Dresden during the Thirty Years' War and spend much of his life between 1633 and 1644 in Denmark. Christian referred to Schütz as 'den sonderbar excellierende und jetziger Zeit fast seines Gleichen nicht habende Musicus' ('the outstanding and almost incomparable musician of his time'). His first commission was to provide music for the marriage of Prince Christian and the Saxon Princess Magdalene Sibylla in 1634, but his contribution to these festivities—probably some kind of opera-ballet—appears to have been lost. The celebrations lasted fourteen days and cost two million *dalers*; they included a banquet lasting six hours to the accompaniment of twenty-four silver trumpets and four kettledrums, and a ballet in which the royal pair danced first, to the regal sound of trumpets and drums, after which the guests danced to a band of strings. The most spectacular event of all was a carousel with more than eighty musicians in attendance, the large Danish forces being augmented by contingents brought by visiting potentates. Schütz may also have written some of his more serious music in Denmark; the second part of his *Geistliche Concerten* (Dresden, 1639) was dedicated to Count Frederik, later Frederik III, and the second part of his *Symphoniae Sacrae* (Dresden, 1647) to Prince Christian.

With the death of Christian IV the splendours of the Danish court began to wane, and war-clouds gathered. Christian IV himself had been defeated by the Swedes in 1644, and his successor Frederik III (1648–70) had to defend Copenhagen against the onslaught of Karl X of Sweden in 1659. The privations of war, the loss of territory and the financial depression that followed the signing of peace between the two countries, led to a reduction in the strength of the chapel choir and in the demise of the ancient trumpeter-corps, whose ceremonial functions were taken over by the cavalry. The court orchestra remained, but its character was altered; Frederik III and his queen, Sophie Amalie, were fond of opera and ballet in the French taste, with string accompaniment. Entertainments of this kind were ordered for every possible occasion, and from 1655 a band of eight 'violins' under a French leader formed the court orchestra; these were styled 'De Kongelige Hofviolons', a title borne by Danish royal instrumentalists until about 1800, when that of 'Kongelige Kapelmusikus' took its place. The court director during Frederik III's reign, Caspar Förster, wrote two sonatas for the ensemble, besides an opera-ballet, *Il Cadmo*, for the betrothal of Princess Anne Sophia to the Crown Prince of Saxony in 1663, and an oratorio, *David og Goliath*, all of which survive in the library of Uppsala University. Under Christian V (1670–99) there was a further decline in the court establishment: the choir or *Cantori* became almost defunct, and even the *Hofviolons* began to melt away as the peaceful enjoyment of music at court entertainments gave way to the clangour of the cavalry trumpets and the strident reed-bands of the foot regiments.[1] But we have the evidence of Le Coffre's vivid ceiling-painting in the Frederiksberg castle,[2] depicting a *Maskarade* in 1704, that under Frederik IV a body of musicians could be assembled for such an occasion; apart from the oriental instruments and the lute which are being played by guests or courtiers, professional performers on harpsichord, oboe, bassoon, violin and cello are visible.

---

[1] The bands of the foot regiments, known as *Skalmeje-Blaesen*, were composed of shawms with alto, tenor and bass pommers, soon to be replaced by oboes and dulcians or bassoons.

[2] See Plate IX.

3

Swedish Music during the
Age of Greatness

With the victorious accession of Gustav Vasa in 1523 and the achievement of full national independence, the career of Sweden as a major European power—the *Stormaktstid*—began. It is true that Gustav's immediate successors were unfortunate rulers; his elder son, Erik XIV, a man of cultured but ill-balanced mind, was soon deposed in favour of his nephew Sigismund, King of Poland, who in turn had to give place to Gustav's youngest son, Karl IX. But the fortunes of the Thirty Years' War, the devastation of so much of Germany, the decline of the Hanseatic towns on the Baltic coasts, and the discomfiture of the Catholic state of Poland, all combined to raise Sweden to the front rank of European politics. Above all, there emerged a national leader of genius both in war and peace: Gustav II Adolf, or Gustavus Adolphus as he is generally called. He reigned from 1611 until 1632, when he was killed before Lützen, leading his army into battle to the singing of the warriors' psalm, *Förfaras ej, du lilla hop*. (See page 52.)

Gustavus Adolphus, like his chief minister Baron Oxenstierna and other prominent members of the court, enjoyed music and invited singers and instrumentalists to Stockholm. The king himself had some skill on the lute; in fact, if he had lived longer he might have rivalled Christian IV of Denmark in his encouragement of the arts. As it was, despite his other interests and responsibilities he left the Swedish court musical establishment in a flourishing state.

The reign of his daughter, the enigmatic Christina, up to her

För - - fä - ras ej, du lil-la hop, Fast fi-en-der-nas
karm och rop Från al - la si - - dor skal - la. De
fröj-das åt din un-der-gång, Men de-ras fröjd ej
bli-ver lång; Ty låt ej mo - - - det fal - - la.

('Fear not, little band, though the enemy's noise and shouting resound on every side. They rejoice at thy destruction, but their joy shall not last long; therefore let not thy courage fail.')[1]

abdication in 1654 brought further enrichment of court life with ballet and pageantry. Artists, musicians, and men of letters from all over Europe were welcomed, but especially from France. The Queen spent lavishly on entertainment; a French ballet, *Les Libéralités des dieux*, presented on her birthday on 8th December 1651 cost 100,000 *riksdaler*. Lively and often amusing observations on various aspects of musical life in Sweden at this time can be found in the journal kept by Bulstrode Whitelocke, Cromwell's ambassador to that country in the years 1653–4.[2]

Whitelocke was a keen amateur musician who had had the advantages of being educated at Merchant Taylors' school. When preparing for his departure to Sweden he saw to it that his official staff and household of nearly a hundred should include several persons capable of taking their parts in vocal and instrumental music, not forgetting two trumpeters for ceremonial occasions, such as the entertainment the ambassador

[1] Verses attributed to Jacob Fabricius (d. 1654); melody of popular German origin.

[2] *Journal of the Swedish Ambassy*, London, 1772, reptd. London, 1855 (Swedish translation 1777).

IX Group of musicians from ceiling painting by Le Coffre (1671–1722) in Frederiksberg Castle, Copenhagen. The painting is said to depict a masquerade held in 1711

X Part of original score of *Drottningholm Music*, by J. H. Roman

gave the Queen on May Day 1654, when she 'highly commended Whitelocke's music of the trumpets, which sounded all supper-time'. She herself dined to the playing of twelve trumpets and kettledrums.[1]

The English visitors particularly admired the royal band with its string section: at a 'masque' (perhaps a ballet) they attended 'the music was excellent, especially the violins, which were many, and rare musicians and fittest for that purpose.' At another court entertainment 'the Queen's music was in a place behind the chair of state—seven or eight violins, with bass viols, flutes and citterns—perfect masters.'[2] In the meantime Whitelocke's own domestic music had not gone unnoticed:

(The Spanish ambassador) staying with Whitelocke above three hours, he was entertained with Whitelocke's music. The *rector chori* was Mr. Ingelo,[3] excellent in that as in other faculties, and seven or eight of his gentlemen, well skilled both in vocal and instrumental music; and Whitelocke himself sometimes in private did bear his part with them, having been in his younger days a master and composer of music. He thought it not unreasonable in the long winter nights to use this recreation, and thereby his people were the better kept together and from disorderly going abroad. (The Ambassador) highly and deservedly commended Whitelocke's music, and acquainted the Queen with it, who was a great lover thereof.[4]

The Queen herself heard a recital of English domestic music a month or so later:

Being returned to the castle at night, she desired to hear Whitelocke's music, whom he sent for to the castle and they played and sang in her presence, wherewith she seemed much pleased, and desired Whitelocke to thank them in her name. She said she never heard so good a concert of music and of English songs, and desired Whitelocke, at his return to England, to procure her some to play on the instruments which would be most agreeable to her.[5]

[1] Op. cit., II, 187, 252.
[2] Op. cit., II 106, I 293.
[3] One of the domestic chaplains.
[4] Op. cit., I, 279.
[5] Op. cit., II, 16.

The Queen's show of interest soon led to an exchange of repertories; on Easter Monday 1654:

> Some of Whitelocke's people went to the castle to hear the Queen's music in her chapel, which they reported to Whitelocke to be very curious. Some Italians of the Queen's music dined with Whitelocke and afterwards sang to him and presented him with a book of their songs, which according to expectation was not unrewarded.

And a few weeks later the Queen's musicians paid a second visit to Whitelocke's household

> with great ceremony to entertain him with their vocal and instrumental music, which was excellent good, and they played many lessons of English composition, which the gentlemen who were musical of Whitelocke's family brought forth unto them.[1]

The English music played on these occasions, and perhaps sent to the Queen at her request, may have included works in contemporary editions now in the university library at Uppsala: the string fancies of Benjamin Rogers, the only extant copy of William Young's sonatas published at Innsbruck in 1653, the 1648 edition of Orlando Gibbons's string fancies, and Thomas Simpson's *Taffelconsort* printed at Hamburg in 1621.

Some of Whitelocke's entries throw light on the state of music in the larger Swedish churches in the middle of the seventeenth century. At Skåra cathedral he observed that 'many scholars were with the masters in upper galleries, singing anthems to the organ and sackbuts'.[2] The English visitors afterwards looked round the choir-school. At Göteborg

> their church musicians were pleased to visit Whitelocke and wondered when they saw him and divers of his people to understand their art, and to sing with them, which they thought had been generally abhorred in England; and were much pleased to find the contrary, but the more with the gratuity he bestowed on them.[3]

At Uppsala the Archbishop considerately ordered 'the music of

[1] Op. cit., II, 64, 135.

[2] Op. cit., I, 187. Owing to the mistranslation of 'sackbuts' by 'sackpibor' in the first Swedish edition, later writers have been led to believe that the accompanying instruments were bagpipes.

[3] Op. cit., I, 161.

the church' to wait on Whitelocke, who was indisposed and perhaps for that reason the more critical:

about twenty persons . . . brought with them their instruments of music, sackbuts, cornets, violins, and did sing and play in his presence reasonably well, although not exactly.'[1]

The Ambassador rewarded the Uppsala musicians with 'forty riksdollars, whereof they were nothing shy in the acceptance; those of Göteborg received only eight *riksdaler* when they came 'about twenty men and boys with lanthorns and candles; . . . and sang in parts, with indifferent good skill and voices; they were choristers, and their music such as they had in their churches.'

Among the Stockholm musicians who entertained Whitelocke, though not named by him, must have been the court director of music, Anders Düben, and probably his brother also, Martin Düben, organist of the Storkyrke. They were sons of Andreas Düben who in 1595 was appointed organist of the Thomaskirche in Leipzig, and both of them had been pupils of Sweelinck before settling in Stockholm. Members of the Düben family were to hold musical posts at church and court under Gustavus Adolphus and his successors for more than a century, and can be regarded as the musician-laureates of the Vasa monarchs.

Among the extant compositions of Anders Düben are dance tunes for strings, representing one side of his court duties: and a motet for double choir, *Pugna triumphalis*, one of the many tributes paid to Gustavus Adolphus, the Lion of the North, after his death in 1632. Düben's motet was written for the re-interment in the Riddarsholmskyrke in 1634; for the earlier memorial service in the German church a threnody, *Defecit gaudium cordis nostri*, for three soloists and male voice choir, was composed by Thomas Boltzius.[2] Anders Düben was still alive in 1660 to compose a *Miserere* for the funeral service of Karl X; the music for this occasion also included a motet by Anders' son and successor, Gustaf Düben.

Gustaf, who became court music director in 1663, may fairly be regarded as the founder of Swedish music. His training had

[1] Op. cit., II, 135.
[2] Later adapted for some unknown reason by Franz Berwald, who replaced the accompanying chorus by one of his own.

been international; he had travelled in France and Germany and was acquainted with Buxtehude. An organ book written in tablature for him in 1641 by his master Caspar Zengel, a court musician and cantor of the German church in Stockholm, contains pieces by Sweelinck, Scheidt, Peter Phillips, John Bull and William Byrd; and a very large collection of *motetti e concerti* which he later compiled includes works by baroque masters associated with the North German towns, Tunder, Ahle, Schütz, Buxtehude and Weckmann, beside compositions by Carissimi and Dumont. Gustaf's original works, now in the Uppsala library, include a *Veni sancte spiritus* for four voices (1651), three symphonies *con cembalo e spinetta* (1654), and a setting of the Lord's Prayer in Swedish, *Fadar vår*, for four voices and five viols, in which the vocal declamation has an impressive strength. In this work Düben had been anticipated by the renowned Italian, Vincenzo Albrici, who while in Queen Christina's service in 1654 produced a polyphonic setting of *Fadar vår* which is the first known religious composition to Swedish words. Gustaf Düben's most ambitious church composition is perhaps his setting of *Surrexit pastor bonus*; but of greater historical and national interest are his monodic songs to secular and sacred words, and in particular the *Odae Sveticae* (1674) to verses by Samuel Columbus, the greatest Swedish lyric poet of the seventeenth century. It is fascinating to observe how Düben approaches the problems of Swedish declamation at almost the same time as Purcell was occupied with the setting of English words:

('What is the world's existence? A shadow, which though without a body is yet like a corpse. Its magnificence? Outward glitter, inward corruption.')

Here the composer is experimenting with expressive declamation; but when, as in some of the *Odae sveticae*, he is content to let the music take control he can achieve a fluent and satisfying melody in the form of a sarabande:

('O how well it is with the soul that continually devotes wit and reason to virtuous conduct, and holds itself firmly thereto, whatever may come. If trouble, even death, assail, it stands, and makes visible the radiance of its happiness.')

Gustaf Düben gave up his post at the German church in 1687, and died three years later. Two of his sons, Gustaf (1659–1726) and Anders (1670–1738) in turn succeeded him at the court, where they attained high rank. Gustaf Düben II entered the service of Prince Karl, the future bellicose Karl XII, and was doubtless expected to provide military music; Mattheson, who spent some time in Stockholm, recalls in his *Grundlage einer Ehrenpforte* (1740) that one could expect to find only *Kriegesmusik* there.[1] Music for entertainment, however, was still not entirely absent from the Swedish capital; in 1699 Anders Düben II composed a ballet in the style of Lully, to be performed by Claude Rosidor's French company, and two years later he contributed to the festivities in honour of the victories of Karl XII.[2] But on the whole the rule of the later Vasa kings was characterized by a decline in arts and letters and a spectacular imperialist expansion. Under Karl X (1654–60) and

[1] It will be recalled that the departure, in 1704, of J. S. Bach's elder brother, Johann Jakob, to serve as oboist under Karl XII, was the occasion for the well-known *Capriccio sopra la lontananza del suo fratello diletissimo*.

[2] The Düben family continued to play a distinguished part in musical life for several more generations, and a Karl Vilhelm Düben was one of the first presidents of the Musical Academy in 1772.

Karl XI (1660–97) the Swedish domains increased until they stretched from the base of the Jutland peninsula in the west to Lake Ladoga in the east, and included not only the whole of the Swedish provinces and islands but also Finland, Esthonia and Livonia. At the turn of the century much of this vast empire was lost through the headstrong adventurousness of Karl XII (1697–1718), and in face of the increasing might of Russia under Peter the Great. With the death of Karl XII the *Stormaktstid* came to an end, and Sweden entered upon a period of political and intellectual reconstruction known as the Age of Freedom (*Frihetstid*).

During the second half of the seventeenth century the university of Uppsala played a very active part in musical life, with the energetic and many-sided Olof Rudbeck (1630–1702) as the moving spirit, both in his student days and during his term of office as Rector. At the age of twenty-one he played the *schalmei*, in the character of a shepherd in a comedy, while the visiting Queen Christina took the role of a chambermaid.[1] Later he designed a new organ for Uppsala cathedral, and composed and directed works on a massive scale with multiple choirs and instrumental groups in the Venetian manner. He supervised the music at the coronations of Karl XI and Karl XII; on the latter occasion the ceremonies were unusually elaborate and have been described for us in a letter written by a contemporary undergraduate to his parents:

> The musicians divided themselves into four choirs, one of which was on the great organ-tribune [presumably the new organ designed by Rudbeck]. The second took its place opposite on a platform built above the altar, the third placed itself on the old organ now in the north transept, and the fourth in a gallery opposite. When the Creed was ended a wonderfully harmonious music was heard from all the choirs of different instruments and voices, which answered one another so sweetly as to give a glimpse of heavenly bliss. But yet that was not to be compared with what followed after the sermon . . . for then was sung the jubilant *O Gud vi lofve tig* [the *Te Deum*] by all the choirs together with pipes and shawms . . . each of the choirs singing its verse in turn round the whole church and responding now nearer, now farther

[1] Norlind, T., *Svensk Folkmusik och Folkdans*. Stockholm, 1930, p. 92.

away with indescribable beauty. . . . After the Benediction the sound of the great organs was heard, and answered by all the choirs with a great number of discant and bass viols, *cymbaler* [harpsichords?], organs, shawms, trumpets and kettledrums.[1]

Another eye-witness describes the thanksgiving service for the victory of Karl XII at Narva in 1700, when the Uppsala students under the direction of Rudbeck, Walerius, Reftelius, and Bellman[2]—all member of the professorial body—provided a choir and orchestra in the cathedral. Again it was the effect of the multiple choirs and orchestras that most impressed the hearers, above all in the *Te Deum* when

Rudbeck began on the new organ, and he and those with him sang the first verse, then the second verse from those at the old organ, and so on . . .

All copies of these imposing compositions seem to have perished in the fire that swept through Uppsala in 1702.

A word must be said about the Professor Walerius, or Vallerius, mentioned in the foregoing account. He not only held the chair of mathematics but was also *director musices* with responsibility for university musical life in general, and cantor for both student and cathedral choirs. He was reputed to be proficient on violin, shawm, dulcian, flute and sackbut, and to be an excellent continuo player. The first complete melody edition of the Swedish psalter, published in 1697, was largely his work. He also wrote a series of monographs on musical subjects: *do sono, de vacuo, de modis,* and *de tactu.*

The growth of urban prosperity and culture in seventeenth-century Sweden raised the status of the town musicians, who now had their guilds and chartered privileges. The town-band of Göteborg, for example, counted among its duties regular playing at church services, at all civic festivities, before proclamations, and on market-days twice a week for the entertainment of the citizens and visitors from the country. As we have seen, the arrival of a distinguished stranger like White-locke gave them an opportunity to give additional recitals and claim financial rewards. The demand for wind-music for the

---

[1] For the sources of this and the following quotation see Moberg: *Från kyrko- och hovmusik till offentlig konsert,* pp. 28–9.

[2] Grandfather of C. M. Bellman.

XI Pages from original score of Gustav Vasa, by J. G. Naumann

POËTEN BELLMAN

XII C. M. Bellman, from the portrait painted for Gustaf III's collection
in 1779 by Pehr Krafft the elder

town-bands led to the importation of repertory, especially from German sources.[1] The sets of occasional verses written for civic and family celebrations mention a variety of instruments in common use: viol, lute, pandora, flute, shawm, cornett or zinck, sackbut (basun), trumpet, and the keyboard instruments —spinet, harpsichord, positive organ, and regal. From similar sources we learn that the older dance-forms—pavane, galliard, sarabande, courante, and gavotte—yielded to newer fashions of French origin—minuet, bourrée, rigaudon and gigue. Side by side with these international dance-rhythms were the popular native dances shared by court, burghers, and peasantry, especially round dances and *polskor*, the latter being a group of dances which seems to have become acclimatized in Sweden during the sixteenth century, when political and commercial ties with Poland were particularly strong. According to White-locke, Queen Christina danced both French and Swedish dances at court; and Karl XI is known to have taken part in a *daldans* while on a visit to Mora in 1673—the earliest historical mention of a Swedish folk-dance.[2]

[1] For example, Hammerschmidt's *Kirchenmusik und Tafelmusik* (1662), Schmeltzer's *Sacroprofanus Concentus* (1662), and Pezel's 40 *Sonatas zum Abblasen um* 10 *Uhr vormittag in Leipzig* (1670).

[2] Norlind, op. cit., p. 148. See, however, the English translation (by J. Streater) of Olaus Magnus, *Historia de Gentibus septentrionalibus* (1555) under the title, *A compendious History of the Goths, Swedes, and Vandals, and other Northern Nations written by Olaus Magnus, Arch-Bishop of Upsall and Metropolitan of Sweden*, published London 1658 with a dedication to 'Sir Bulstrode Whitlock, Late Lord Ambassador to the Court of Sweden'. The following description occurs in Bk. XV, Ch. 8:

'There is also another Exercise for young men. . . . For first, being included in circles or rings, they sing modestly the Deeds of famous men, and with Pipes or Drums playing they go round, and turn back again, by the word only of him that is the Leader, whom they call the King. Then loosing their round rings, they make a little more speed, and by a mutual inclination (as they did before with their sword) they make a *Rosa*, that they may appear in a sexagular figure. And that this may be done more solemnly, and with greater noise, they bind little brass bells to tinckle at their knees, like Morris-dancers.'

Additional note Norlind, in *Från tyska kyrkans glansdagar*, III, pp. 144 seq. (Stockholm 1945), draws attention to the compositions of Christian Geist, court organist at Stockholm from 1670 to 1679, and thereafter a leading organist in Copenhagen until his death in 1711. Geist's works include three elaborate cantatas for 5-part choir, soloists and orchestra, evidently intended for state occasions in the Swedish royal chapel.

4

Two Scandinavian Masters of the Baroque: Didrik Buxtehude and Johan Helmich Roman

We have seen that during the first half of the seventeenth century the Danish court fostered a short-lived native school of composers, represented chiefly by Mogens Pedersøn and Hans Nielsen, who were on the whole content to follow in the wake of the early baroque Flemish, German, and Italian polyphonists. Before the end of the same century, however, a Scandinavian composer had appeared whose roots were in the religious and secular musical life of Denmark and southern Sweden, but whose versatility and originality were to give him far wider influence, spreading throughout northern Germany and inspiring both Handel and J. S. Bach.

Neither the date nor the place of birth of Didrik (or Dietrich) Buxtehude are precisely known. The family name comes from the town between Bremen and Hamburg, but it is generally believed that the composer was born in 1637 in Helsingborg, in the province of Skåne which is now Swedish but was then under Danish rule. At the time of Didrik's birth his father was organist of the Mariakyrke in Helsingborg: but after a few years the family crossed the Sound to Helsingør, the father having been appointed to the Olaikirke there, a post he was to hold until 1671. With Kronborg castle in the background, it is more than likely that the boy came into contact with the music of Frederik III's court, diminished though it was from the splendours of Christian IV. In 1657 Didrik became organist of his father's former church in Helsingborg, and three years later gained the more responsible appointment at the Mariakirke in Helsingør; the façade of the organ as he knew it[1] and the house where he is believed to have lived, are both preserved in Helsingør.

In 1668 Buxtehude succeeded Franz Tunder at the Marien-kirche in Lübeck, where he served not only as organist but also as *Werkmeister,* an office entailing a wide range of duties connected with the archives, the finances, and the general upkeep and administration of the church fabric and services. Buxtehude was to remain in Lübeck until his death in 1707, building up a wide reputation as executant, choirmaster, and composer, and forming a living historical link between the great organists of the early baroque—Sweelinck and Schütz—and the young Handel and Bach, both of whom visited the organ-loft in the Marienkirche: Handel in 1703 in company with Mattheson,[2] who had hopes of becoming Buxtehude's successor, and Bach in 1705, on leave from Arnstadt to attend the Advent-tide *Abendmusik* instituted eight years earlier. Other disciples of Buxtehude were Vincent Lübeck, later organist in Hamburg, and Nikolaus Bruhns who became organist of the Nikolaikirke in Copenhagen, where he is said to have displayed the unusual accomplishment of performing trio-sonatas by playing the upper parts on the violin in double-stopping, while adding the bass on the organ pedals.

Although Buxtehude spent the longest and most productive part of his career outside Scandinavian territories, he remained in close touch with Denmark and Sweden. Besides sending at least one brilliant pupil to a Danish post, he seems to have been on terms of friendship with Gustaf Düben in Sweden, and the Swedish libraries are rich in original manuscripts, or transcripts of his works. Of great interest also is a series of keyboard suites and variations which came to light at Nykøbing in 1939, after having been in the custody of descendants of Johan Christian Ryge (1688–1758), cantor of Roskilde cathedral in Denmark.

[1] Photograph reproduced in Vol. I of Josef Hedar's edtn. of the *Organ Works* (W. Hansen, 1952).
[2] For Mattheson's singular contribution to Scandinavian musicology, see Appendix II, and facsimile (Plate XV).

This manuscript,[1] noted in tablature, includes two sets of variations on tunes known to have been popular in Scandinavia in the late seventeenth century.[2] Another recent discovery was made (also in 1939) by Josef Hedar in the library of Lund University; it consists of a collection of organ works handed down through a succession of pupils.[3] While some of these pieces may belong to Buxtehude's early career in Helsingør, the only work that bears definite evidence of having been composed before Buxtehude's departure to Lübeck is the cantata, *Aperite mihi portas iustitiae*, in the manuscript of which the composer is described as 'ecclesiae quae Helsingorae est Germanicae organista'.

This is not the place to attempt a full appreciation of Buxtehude's achievement as a composer, which lies in three main fields: keyboard works for organ and harpsichord, trio sonatas,[4] and church cantatas.[5] In all three he was brilliant and often daring, and when at his best shows an eloquence and depth of feeling that even Handel and J. S. Bach hardly surpass. In his organ toccatas, chaconnes, and chorale preludes, as well as in the newly-discovered harpsichord suites,[6] he gives play to an exuberant and sometimes wayward fancy that seems to spring from some inherent trait in the Danish temperament, and reappears in modern times in the work of Carl Nielsen. The parallel may perhaps be brought out by juxtaposing two passages by Buxtehude, the one from the closing bars of the organ prelude on *Wie schön leuchtet der Morgenstern*, with its remarkable suspensions, and the other from a *ciacona*: and an

---

[1] Published in a critical edition by Emilius Bangert (Hansen), 1942.

[2] One of these is the folk-tune known in Germany as *Kraut und Rüben* and introduced by J. S. Bach into the quodlibet at the end of the *Goldberg Variations*; the other is a ballet tune of French origin, set by Kingo in *Aandelige Sjungekor* (1674) to the psalm 'Rind nu op i Jesu navn'.

[3] A page of tablature from this collection is reproduced in Vol. I of Hedar's edition of the organ works (Hansen). Each of the four volumes of this edition contains a photograph of one of the North German or Scandinavian organs associated with Buxtehude.

[4] Several of the trio sonatas have been edited by Wenziger (Bärenreiter).

[5] Many of the solo and choral cantatas are available in practical modern editions (Bärenreiter).

[6] A critical account of the keyboard suites is given by Kathleen Dale in an article in *The Listener* (10th July, 1952).

excerpt from Carl Nielsen's large-scale organ piece *Commotio*, dating from 1932:

Buxtehude, *Wie schön leuchtet der Morgenstern*

Buxtehude, *Ciacona*

(a)   Carl Nielsen, *Commotio*

Finally, a brief quotation from the cantata *Alles was ihr tut* may serve to illustrate the popular cast of much of Buxtehude's sacred music, especially that produced in connection with the *Abendmusiken* and therefore intended to combine spiritual edification with a legitimate degree of entertainment for the tired business men of Lübeck:

('All that ye do, in words or in deeds, do it in Jesus' name.')

Vocal writing such as this, simple, tuneful, and extrovert, seems to spring from the gentle contours of the Danish landscape and to point onwards to a tradition of popular choral song associated with the names of Kuhlau, Weyse, Gade, and Nielsen.

To the aged and revered Buxtehude, the young Handel was only one of the many admirers who called on him in Lübeck to study his organ-playing and composition, and perhaps to assess their chances of succeeding to his appointment. To Johan Helmich Roman, who was in his early teens when Buxtehude died, Handel appeared as the greatest of living composers, to be sought out during student days in England and later introduced through his works to the courtiers and citizens of Sweden. Roman grew up during the last phase of the Swedish Age of Greatness. His father was a member of the court band in Stockholm, and his godfather was the younger Gustaf Düben. As a junior court musician he must have taken part in the rejoicing over the victories of Karl XII and the mourning over the disaster at Poltava in 1709 and the King's death in 1718.

These events had direct repercussions on the fortunes of musicians, since the French theatre company was sent home and the royal orchestra was no longer called upon to play at elaborate church services of thanksgiving. The political scene was transformed. Karl XII's sister, Ulrika-Eleonora, who came to the throne in 1718, handed over the reins of government two years later to her husband, Frederic of Hesse-Cassel, and with him, under his title of Fredrik I of Sweden, accepted constitutional limitations of the royal power. By the peace of Nystad in 1721 Sweden ceded her East Baltic possessions to Russia, and turned inwards to the task of reorganizing trade and public administration. This was the beginning of the Age of Freedom (*Frihetstid*), a liberal régime not only in politics and religion but also in scientific thought and in the arts. The eighteenth century in Sweden saw the rise of the national scientific and literary academies; it was the age of Carl Linnaeus (1707–1778), the great botanist, and of Emmanuel Swedenborg (1688–1772), who also was an original scientific investigator but is remembered chiefly as a religious mystic. In literature, the Augustan writers of England and the poets and philosophers of the French age of enlightenment were taken as models, and soon a constellation of native Swedish poets arose, all owing allegiance to Boileau and his ideals of clarity, good sense, and the harmonious use of language. It was at this period that the beauty of the Swedish tongue was fully realized and revealed.

Gifted not only as a practical musician but also as a linguist, Roman moved easily among the cultured circles of Swedish society. His talents attracted the attention of Queen Ulrika-Eleonora, who sent him to England to study with J. C. Pepusch (1667–1752), the German-born violinist, composer and theoretician who had settled in London about the turn of the century and was later to become partly responsible for the success of *The Beggar's Opera*. A set of attractive sonatas of his for violin and figured bass exists in the library of Uppsala university, and has appeared in a modern edition,[1] while his textbook of harmony was translated into Swedish by Roman himself. Other outstanding musicians whom Roman met in England included Geminiani, Buononcini, and in all probability Handel. On his return to Stockholm in 1720 Roman was appointed deputy director of music at court, and almost at once found himself confronted with the problem of arranging suitable music for the coronation of Fredrik I with a bare handful of orchestral players. Nine years later, when he succeeded the younger Anders Düben as chief court musician, he set about the task of

[1] Edtd. Degen and Lenzewski, Schott Edition 3631.

raising the royal band to a size and standard of proficiency it had never known before. Roman was himself a fine violinist and oboist, and he inspired enthusiasm throughout the capital, so that in his later years he could assemble on occasion an orchestra of 140 players, mostly amateurs from Stockholm and neighbourhood with the professional stiffening of the royal band. In 1731 he started a series of *concerts spirituels*, the first public concerts ever to be given in Sweden.

Roman displayed his interest in the possibilities of the Swedish language as a medium for lyric and dramatic poetry and song by translating the texts of some of Handel's works, including the *Brockes Passion* (to which he added Swedish chorales), *Esther*, and *Acis and Galatea*; by composing a setting of the Swedish Mass and a *Jubilate* in the vernacular; and by adapting to Swedish words compositions by Lassus, Carissimi, Lotti and other Italian masters. In recognition of his services to the cause of the Swedish language, as well as to his position as the 'father of Swedish music', he was elected in 1740 a member of the Royal Academy of Sciences.

Although Roman's style as a composer was modelled on that of Handel it bears its own stamp of personality. Instrumental works occupy the most prominent place; some of it was intended for court occasions, like the so-called *Drottningholm Music*,[1] a set of twenty-four pieces written for a royal wedding, but much of the chamber music, like the sonatas for two violins and bass,[2] was probably designed to meet the growing demand for an amateur domestic repertory. Among the works of this kind is a set of twelve *Sonate a Flauto traverso, violone e cembalo* published in 1727 with a dedication to the Queen. There are numerous sinfonias and concertos for chamber orchestra, the partita in C minor for oboe, strings and continuo being of special historical interest, as a work by Handel for the same combination, and dating from the period when Roman was in England, exists in manuscript in the Uppsala library.[3]

---

[1] See facsimile, Plate X.

[2] Edtd. in two volumes by Patrik Vretblad, Carl Gehrmans Musik-förlag, Stockholm.

[3] Roman's sinfonia has been published in a modern edition by Hilding Rosenberg (Carl Gehrmans Musikförlag). The Roman manuscripts in the library of the Royal Musical Academy in Stockholm include two sets of

Roman is a fine craftsman, lacking except on rare occasions the magnificent sweep of Handel's imagination, but often showing a subtlety of rhythmic organization that is all his own. The following passage, from the sixth of the 7 *Sonate a tre*, is an example of his expressive power and sense of instrumental effect:

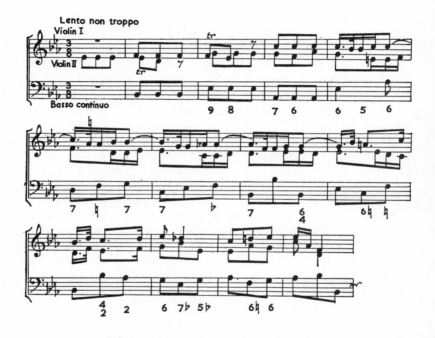

A short excerpt from the Swedish *Jubilate* will serve to show not only how Roman handles the declamation of his native tongue, but also how idiomatically he uses instruments in allusion to the pastoral metaphor:

sonate a tre and ten 'trios', bringing the total extant number of works in this form up to seventeen. See Bengtsson, I., *J. H. Roman och hans instrumental-musik*, Uppsala, 1955 (with English summary).

('He hath made us for his people and the sheep of his pasture.')

Roman stands near the end of the baroque age in Swedish music. Changes of taste were going on during his lifetime; the German-born King Adolf Fredrik and his Queen Lovisa-Ulrika preferred the modish *galant* style in the arts, and had a particular liking for opera-ballet in the French taste. Interest in the concerto grosso, in the trio sonata, and in elaborate settings for church use dwindled. After Roman's death, which occurred in 1758, his achievements were forgotten, and even his name was scarcely known until the rediscovery and revival that came in the first half of the twentieth century. It was then that Swedish musicians realized with delight that they not only possessed an ancestor of some stature, but also that they could adopt his work as one of the foundations of a modern Swedish school, with its anti-romantic, neo-baroque sympathies.

5

The Foundations of Scandinavian Opera

Although the sixteenth century has its school plays with interpolated songs, and the seventeenth its imported interludes and opera-ballet, the history of opera in the Scandinavian countries only begins in earnest in the last quarter of the seventeenth century.

The first Danish opera house, a small wooden structure put up near the Charlottenburg palace for a performance in honour of the birthday of King Christian V in 1689[1] was burnt down a few days later with terrible loss of life; but a more substantial building was opened in the Grønnegade in 1722, when Reinhard Keiser brought his opera company from Hamburg and composed his *Ulysses* expressly for the Danish stage. Another important visitor was Gluck, who included Copenhagen and Christiania in his tour with Pietro Mingotti's Italian troupe between 1747 and 1750; but in spite of the patronage of Queen Lovisa, who admired Italian opera and had at one time been a pupil of Handel, the company suffered financial loss and came to an end in 1756, its last director being Giuseppe Sarti, whose son (of the same name) was to become a leading figure in Danish musical life.

Italian opera had a formidable opponent in the great Norwegian-born dramatist Ludvig Holberg (1684–1754), sometimes called 'the Molière of the North'. Holberg had a musical

[1] The work performed was *Der vereinigte Götterstreit*, with German text by P. A. Burckhardt and music, which has not survived, by P. C. Schindler, one of the *Hofviolons*.

bent, and helped to support himself while a student at Oxford by giving lessons on the recorder; and like Molière, some of whose comedies also were played on the Grønnegade stage, Holberg provided scope for musical situations with songs, dances and instrumental interludes. His *Kilderejsen* is a skit on Keiser's Hamburg opera, with a heroine who is unable to speak naturally and must express herself entirely in trills.

From 1748 the rebuilt royal opera house at Charlottenburg, where the French and Italian companies gave their performances, had a competitor in the new Komediehus in the Kongens Nytorv, where the Royal Theatre now stands. Here the comedies of Holberg formed the core of the repertory, together with numerous *syngestykker*, or comedies with songs and dances to tunes borrowed chiefly from French and German sources and arranged by Carl August Thielo, a busy playwright, critic, and composer of light music. In response to a popular demand for the publication of favourite airs from Thielo's productions, a collection appeared in print in 1751.[1] The marriage of Danish texts to foreign tunes became a profitable occupation, and among those who were quick to exploit it was the younger Giuseppe Sarti, who soon learnt to adapt his native Italian style to the requirements of Danish comedy. In 1756 he drew upon arias from his own operas in setting a libretto on a Danish subject, *Gram og Signe*, by the Norwegian writer Niels Krog Bredal, new recitatives being written by another composer familiar with the Danish language. Bredal and Sarti collaborated again in a piece entitled *Tronfølgen i Sidon* ('The succession in Sidon') which was chiefly remarkable for touching off a 'war of the theatres' out of which emerged one of the classics of the Danish stage.

The text of *Kjærlighed uden Strømper* ('Love without stockings') was by Johan Herman Wessel (1742–1785), whose aim was to parody the conventions of French classical drama; the music imitates the style of Sarti, and was composed by Paolo Scalabrini, another Italian resident in Copenhagen who had formerly been court music director. The outrageous plot, culminating in a series of suicides, whereupon Mercury

---

[1] *Første Samling af de Oder som paa den danske Skueplads udi København er blevne opførte.*

descends to revive the corpses, and the absurdly inflated text with its extravagant similes, are matched by the elaborate arias put into the mouths of a tailor, a maidservant and other low-life characters. The satirical intention and effect are reminiscent of *The Beggar's Opera*, though the technical means are different. It is not certain whether Scalabrini was deliberately carica-turing Sarti, or whether he knew too little Danish to realize the incongruity of his settings. In either case, his flamboyant writing brought out the full absurdity of arias beginning:

'As an unlucky skipper, who sees he must be wrecked on one of two cliffs and cannot choose which it shall be, so am I . . .' and

'In the fireplace of my heart a sooty flame is burning, lit at both ends.'

Wessel's brilliant satire did little, however, to detract from Sarti's prestige in Copenhagen. From 1770, while he was still court musical director, he had been placed in charge also of the music at the Komediehus, and undertook the task of providing the capital with a first-class operatic orchestra. He achieved his aim by combining the court band or *Hofviolons* with the court musicians of Plön, a dukedom that had reverted to the crown of Denmark, and also engaged some eminent players from other countries. The total strength of the orchestra as Sarti left it was fourteen strings, two flutes, two oboes, two bassoons and two horns, and from that time the senior orchestra of the Danish capital (Det Kgl. Kapel) has been firmly linked with the Royal Theatre. One of the players who came from Plön has a niche of his own in Danish musical history; this was Johan Ernst Hartmann (1726–93), leader of the orchestra for a quarter of a century and one of the most important figures in the Scandinavian romantic movement.

In Sweden operatic development was following much the same course as in Denmark, leading from imported entertain-ments to the foundation of a national school. At the beginning of the period French influence was paramount; its extent can be judged from the large collection of scores dating from the time of Karl XII in the Uppsala University library. No fewer than fifty-two operas by sixteen different composers, including Lully himself, are extant from the period between 1699 and 1707, when Claude de Rosidor directed a French company season after season in the Swedish capital.[1] Not until 1747 was an operatic work produced with a Swedish text; it was a three-act *opéra-comique* entitled *Syrinx eller Den uti vass förvandlade vattnymphen* ('Syrinx or the water-nymph changed into a reed'), with libretto by Lars Lalin and music put together from works by Handel, Graun and others.

As already noticed, the accession of Adolf Fredrik and Lovisa-Ulrika in 1751 led to renewed interest in French *opéra-comique*, with a repertory made up of works by Monsigny, Phildor, Grétry and others, those of Grétry becoming especially popular through the influence of Gustaf Filip Creutz, poet and Swedish ambassador to Paris. But the King and Queen also gave their patronage to Italian opera, and at their invitation Francesco Uttini (1723–95) who had been associated with Gluck, introduced a series of works with libretti by Metastasio dealing with classical subjects: *Il Re pastore*, *L'Eroe cinese*, *Adriano in Siria*, and *Thetis och Pelée*, to which Uttini added Swedish recitatives, for the inauguration of a new opera house in 1773. Three theatres were now available: the new one in Bollhuset, to which the general public were admitted, and two court theatres: the one in the Drottningholm palace, designed by C. F. Adelcrantz and opened in 1766, still exists with its machinery and some of the original sets.[2]

The opening of the public opera house in Stockholm marked the beginning of the Gustavian age, during which for twenty years all the theatre arts enjoyed a halcyon period under the protection of King Gustaf III (1772–1792). The King was an enthusiastic amateur actor and dramatic author and had an almost mystical belief in the value of the drama in the life of a nation. He maintained the Drottningholm theatre on an even more lavish scale than his predecessors, with a great deal of ballet and spectacle in the French style and with the best Italian singers he could engage. In 1782 he presided over the opening of yet another new theatre partly designed by himself and placed under the direction of a high court official. This theatre was intended to serve as a training school for actors and singers in the Swedish language, which was henceforward to be used in

[1] Moberg, op. cit., p. 43.
[2] The theatre in the Ulriksdal palace dates from 1753 and yet a third, at Gripsholm, was built in 1782.

preference to French and Italian. The King also founded the Royal Academy of Music (Kungliga Musikaliska Akademien) in 1771 with a charter to promote 'all that appertained to musical scholarship' and to provide training in both theoretical and practical branches of the art. Out of this institution the present Stockholm Conservatory (Kungliga Musikhogskolen) developed in the nineteenth century. Every opera-goer knows how the theatre that had been the focus of Gustaf III's dreams and experiments provided the setting for his death when on the night of 16th March 1792 the King was struck down by an assassin's bullet, thereby creating in his last moments one more opera plot—that of Verdi's *Un Ballo in Maschera*. The Gustavian Age and the last remnants of the Swedish empire, since the new King Gustaf IV became involved in war with Russia, lost the principality of Finland and the Åland Islands, and was forced by his generals to abdicate.

A central figure in the story of Gustavian opera, John Gottlieb Naumann (1741–1801) was active in both Stockholm and Copenhagen.[1] Naumann's Scandinavian career began in 1778, when he came from Dresden to produce his *Amphion* in Swedish on the Stockholm stage. Four years later he wrote *Cora och Alonzo* for the opening of the King's new opera house, and in 1786 made Swedish operatic history by producing *Gustaf Vasa*,[2] the first Swedish opera on a national subject. The libretto was by the celebrated poet and amateur musician, J. H. Kellgren, who worked, it was said, on a prose draft prepared by the King.

Naumann rose to the occasion with a work that excels in sense of theatre, in declamation, and above all in a masterly treatment of the orchestra: for example, during Gustaf's *recitativo a tempo* in the second Act ('Now at last I may let my pent-up tears flow freely'), which is accompanied by flutes, horns, bassoons, and strings, with a 'retreat' of fifes, clarinets, trumpets, and drums sounding off-stage and a soft drum-roll continuing throughout; and in the ghost scene in Act III, where

---

[1] See Engländer, R., *J. G. Naumann als Opernkomponist*, 1922, an appendix to which contains excerpts from *Gustaf Vasa* and *Orfeus*; also the same author's *Joseph Martin Kraus und die Gustavianische Oper*, Uppsala, 1943–4.
[2] See Plate XI.

violas, bassoons and bass trombone are used with telling skill.[1]

In the same year, Naumann made a notable contribution to the Danish operatic stage, producing in Copenhagen the first grand opera to a Danish text (by C. D. Biehl) entitled *Orfeus og Eurydice*. The Danish court was still seeking for a successor to Sarti and Scalabrini, both of whom had by this time left Denmark, and the opportunity to appoint Naumann to the post of director at the Royal Theatre was eagerly grasped. He was thus able to continue Sarti's work in building up the Danish orchestra (Det Kgl. Kapel).[2]

The success of Naumann's *Gustaf Vasa* set a fashion in Sweden for operas and *sångspelar* (musical plays) on national subjects. One of the first to exploit it was J. G. Vogler ('The Abbé Vogler') who toured Sweden between 1786 and 1799, giving organ recitals and supervising the building of organs. He was appointed director of the Royal Theatre in 1786 and composed a *sångspel* entitled *Gustav Adolf och Ebba Brahe* to a text by Kellgren. The versatile Carl Stenborg, who had a reputation as actor, antiquary, historian, and singer, produced two similar works, *Gustav Adolfs Jakt* (1777) and *Gustav Vasa in Dalarna* (1787), the latter being the first Swedish opera to introduce traditional Swedish melodies.

In Denmark also operatic subjects were taken from national history and legends: Kunzen's *Holger Danske* (1789) and *Erik Ejegod* (1795) are examples. But in general Danish operatic taste at the turn of the century showed a preference for homelier characterization and for simple strophic song related to popular or folk music. Thus J. A. P. Schultz collaborated with Thomas Thaarup in two idealized pictures of Zealand peasant life: *Høstgildet* ('The harvest feast') (1790) and *Peters Bryllup* ('Peter's wedding') (1793), with songs that recall the more artless examples of the English ballad opera. Other successful works of a similar kind were produced by F. L. Æ. Kunzen at the begin-

---

[1] The orchestra of the new opera house in 1782 included 16 violins (in addition to the leader), 5 violas, 4 cellos, 4 basses, 4 flutes, 3 oboes, 2 clarinets, 2 bassoons, 2 trumpets and timpani.

[2] The standards of this orchestra were maintained under Naumann's successors: J. A. P. Schultz, F. L. Æ. Kunzen, Edouard Du Puy, and the Danish-born Claus Nielsen Schall, in whose time it gave the first performance of Weber's *Freischütz* overture at a concert directed by the composer in 1820.

ning of his term of office as director of the Royal Theatre; his *syngespil* entitled *Dragedukken* ('The puppet') (1795), dealing with the fortunes of a Copenhagen cobbler, held the stage for thirty-five years. Yet another classic of *syngespil* was the work of Edouard Du Puy who, on an occasion when the material for a performance of Méhul's *opéra-comique, Une folie*, failed to arrive, reset the Danish adaptation of Bouilly's text under the title of *Ungdom og Galskab* ('Youth and madness') (1806).

The beginnings of the romantic period of Danish opera came about through the partnership of the poet Johannes Ewald (1743–81) and J. E. Hartmann, who collaborated in 1779 in the production of *Balders Død* ('The death of Balder'), a *syngespil* based on Norse legend and with one remarkable anticipation of Wagner's Valkyrie music:

('Nastrond's flames roar thunderously; deep are the emotions of the maid of Valhalla.')

The chief interest of *Fiskerne* ('The fishermen') which Ewald and Hartmann produced in 1780 lies in the introduction of the first stanza of the Danish national song, *Kong Christian stod ved højen Mast* ('King Christian stood beside the tall mast'), though the tune now associated with Ewald's ballad about Christian IV is not found in the original version of *Fiskerne*, but soon after the production of that work became popular and was attributed to Hartmann. It is still uncertain whether it was his own composition or was adapted by him from a traditional source. But whatever share Hartmann may have had in its creation, most of the credit for realizing the excellence of the tune and for putting it into a worthy setting is due to Friedrich Kuhlau, who after composing a set of variations on it introduced the whole melody twice into one of the most attractive and historically important stage works of the Danish romantic period, the *syngespil Elverhøj* ('The fairy hill') (1828). The tune occurs first as the climax of the overture and again in the final chorus. The sturdy harmony and brilliant figuration of the passage in the overture provide one of the most stirring moments in Danish orchestral music:

This apotheosis of the Danish national song is not the only claim of *Elverhøj* for admiration. The libretto was the work of Johan Ludvig Heiberg (1791–1860), a poet, dramatist and critic, and the occasion of its first performance in November 1828 was a royal betrothal, when a combination of patriotic sentiment and the prevailing taste for the romantically supernatural was obviously appropriate. Heiberg was one of the leading exponents of national romanticism, and it was probably at his suggestion that Kuhlau took some of the tunes for his *syngespil* from the collections of folk melodies that were being published during the first two decades of the nineteenth century.[1] How sensitively Kuhlau used this material can be seen in the following passage from the vocal score of *Elverhøj*;

Jeg lag-de mit Ho - ved til El - ver - høj, mi-ne Ø-jer de fin-ge en Dvale; da kom mig i-mø-de Jom-fru-er to, og lok-ked mig med Sang og med Tvi - le: E - ia, hvor sel-som en Dands!

[1] See page 89.

('I laid my head on Fairy Hill, my eyes closed in a trance; then two maidens came to meet me and enchanted me with song and bewilderment. Ah, how strange a dance.')

Heiberg is remembered not only as the librettist of *Elverhøj* but also for his share in introducing the *vaudeville* into Denmark, and for writing the texts of a number of works in this form, which differed from the *syngespil* chiefly through the greater pungency of its satire and through the closer connection it observed between dramatic situation and song; the music, however, was seldom original, but might be taken from almost any source—the operas of Mozart and Weber, popular tunes of unknown origin, and earlier stage music. Both *syngespil* and vaudeville remained in fashion until the last quarter of the nineteenth century, when they were engulfed by the operettas of Offenbach and by musical comedy. Vaudeville songs by the dozen were printed in collections of student songs and established themselves in the popular repertory.

In the meantime true folksong had begun to find its way into the musical plays of Denmark's neighbours. As early as 1814 the author A. Fryxell had used the beautiful Swedish *Värmlandsvisan* ('Song of Värmland') in his folk play *Värmlandsflicka* ('The girl of Värmland'); and in 1824, four years before the production of *Elverhøj*, the Norwegian musician Waldemar Thrane (1790–1838) introduced into a concert performance of Bjerregaard's *Fjaeldeventyret* ('The mountain story')[1] a traditional Norwegian melody that foreshadowed Solveig's song in *Peer Gynt*:

So-le gaar bak Aa-se ne;— Skug-gjin bli saa lan - ge:

Naat-te kjem snart at - te - ve,— te - ke me i Fan-gje.

Kry - tre ·u — ti Kvi - enn staar,— e aat Sae-ter-stul - le gaar.

[1] Produced for the first time on the stage in 1850, in Christiania. A performance was given in Bergen in 1851, and others soon afterwards in Copenhagen and Stockholm.

('The sun goes behind the mountains, the shadows grow long; night falls swiftly, takes me captive. The heifers stand in the byre, and I go to the saeter-hut.')

Before ending this chapter we must refer to a fascinating personality in Swedish music who, though primarily a lyricist, had some connection with opera and whose talent and temperament make him almost a symbol of the Gustavian Age. Carl Michael Bellman (1740–1795)[1] was a man of good family and education; at various times of his life he held official posts under the protection and favour of Gustaf III, and moved in court circles as easily as among the taverns of Stockholm, which he frequented, guitar in hand, to sing the gently satirical verses for which he was renowned. At first he followed the tradition of parody that had grown up in seventeenth-century Sweden: parody of Bible stories, and later parody of the elaborate and rather pompous ritual that accompanied the functions of the upper and middle class orders, societies and clubs. Bellman carried this schoolboy humour into the realm of artistry; he was a master of poetic metres, and had an ear for a good tune which he would borrow from the theatre or the club-room and adapt to his own purposes, so that it was often difficult for his friends to decide whether he had altered a melody to fit his verses or had composed the verses according to the pattern of a melody he happened to like. Above all, Bellman had a warm heart for humanity and a real love of the natural scenery around Stockholm. He invented his own gallery of characters—Fredman, the picaresque clockmaker, 'without clocks, shop, or business', Ulla Winblad of easy virtue, Movitz the musician laden with a miscellany of instruments and misfortunes, and these appear and reappear in Bellman's collections of songs— *Fredmans Epistlar och Sångar* (1790) and its sequel, *Fredmans Sångar* (1791)—drinking, going for picnics, escaping from fires, giving extempore concerts, and attending one another's funerals, all in a setting of the Stockholm streets and suburbs that is half realistic, half idealistic in the eighteenth-century theocritan and anacreontic conventions.

The Bellman songs are full of musical references; there are directions for the singer to imitate the horn, the 'cello, the

[1] See Plate XII.

clarinet, the flute, the bassoon, the trumpet or the drum—or perhaps for the actual instruments to be heard, for some of the songs are extended almost to the dimensions of miniature cantatas.[1] Not all of Bellman's tunes have been identified, but they are known to include adaptations from Italian opera, French *opéra-comique*, instrumental minuets and other pieces, as well as Swedish folk-songs, marches, and *polskor*.[2] Two examples only can be quoted here. The first, to a tune of minuet-like character and probably of French origin, was sung in Bellman's *sångspel Fiskarne* ('The fishermen') in 1773; the verses were written in the country south of Stockholm a few months earlier:

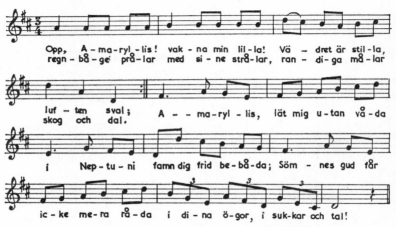

('Up, Amaryllis, wake, my little one. The weather is calm, the air cool: the rainbow displays its radiance, its colours painting wood and dale. Amaryllis, let me invite you without fear to Neptune's bosom; the god of sleep shall not reign longer over your eyes, in your sighing and your speaking.')

The second example is a mock funeral ode set to the tune of *La Folia*, the sarabande of unknown provenance that became common property among composers of the seventeenth and eighteenth centuries:

---

[1] The musical settings were probably elaborated by Olof Ahlstrom, a pupil of Zellbell who edited the two *Fredman* books and between 1789 and 1823 published songs of his own entitled *Skaldestycker satta i musik*.

[2] Afzelius, A., *Bellmans Melodier*, Stockholm, 1947.

('See the black waves' white scum, and see how Charon
struggles. He wrings the water from his beard and labours with
his boat. He tries to beat the waves with his oars, but the
billows strike back; heaven's windows stand open and all the
clouds are bursting.')

Bellman has been called an eighteenth-century troubadour,
and it is certainly difficult to find his counterpart in any modern
literature of verse and song. He has many of the qualities,
though not the range of imagination and sympathy, of Robert
Burns, and the comparison, imperfect thought it must be, may
give some idea of the place of affection that Bellman holds in
Sweden and, to some extent, in the other Scandinavian

countries. Like Burns, he has given rise to a specialist critical literature and a society exists to do him honour. He has enriched Scandinavian song with lyrics of genius and with a store of melodies which, however they originated, will always be associated with his name.

6

National Romanticism and the
Study of Folk Music

Well before the beginning of the nineteenth century the Scandinavian lands and peoples had established a position of special importance amid the cross-currents of literary and artistic ideas that are collectively known as the romantic revival. The reasons for this were threefold. First, the northern races were the acknowledged heirs and custodians of the great system of Nordic mythology that was being revealed to creative artists as a fresh store of inspiring material to replace the over-worked legends and history of Greece and Rome. Secondly, the remoteness, mystery and grandeur of the Scandinavian peninsula and the rich culture of its peasant communities kindled the romantic imagination. And thirdly, the northern countries showed a proud spirit of independent nationalism, and their comparative insignificance in the political economy of Napoleonic Europe only threw into higher relief their struggles to recall and revive the sturdy qualities of their ancestors and to translate these into terms of representative and constitutional government.

In Scandinavia, as in Germany and England, poets and antiquarians joined forces in their search for the past. The beginning of the romantic movement in Denmark can even be given a precise date—that of the publication of Oehlenschläger's famous poem, *Guldhornerne*, an evocation of the legendary past inspired by the discovery, and subsequent loss, of two golden horns that may have been musical instruments of the *lur* family. Adam Oehlenschläger (1779–1850), who wrote the poem in

1802, followed at first in the footsteps of Schiller, Klopstock and other German romantics, but eventually became the leader of a distinctive Danish school that included in its range of subject-matter not only Danish history and the lore of the mediaeval ballads, but also Old Norse literature—the eddas and sagas to which Johannes Ewald directed his countrymen's attention. Oehlenschläger's Swedish contemporaries were Erik Gustav Geijer (1783–1847) and Esaias Tegnér (1782–1846), professor of Greek at Lund and later Bishop of Växjö. In 1811 Tegnér wrote a cantata text, *Svea*, alluding to the loss of Finland as a Swedish possession three years earlier, and in 1829, at a ceremony in Lund cathedral, he acclaimed Oehlenschläger as a brother-poet and the 'King of Scandinavian Song'.

Among those who helped to spread romantic ideas in Denmark was N. F. S. Grundtvig (1783–1872), a remarkable personality who is honoured in his country's history as scholar, philosopher, poet and, above all, educationist. He wrote a vast amount of religious and secular verse, much of it adapted to traditional tunes, and his hymns and songs became an integral part of Danish popular culture.[1] In Sweden, on the other hand, romanticism made its way more slowly into the lives of the people; it was centred in university life at Uppsala and the literary coteries known (from the name of their journal) as *Fosforister* whose idealistic tendencies found expression in the poetic drama *Lycksalighetens Ö* ('The Isle of Bliss') written in the 1820s by P. D. A. Atterbom (1790–1855). Geijer, whom we have already mentioned, was another member of this circle, and a versatile scholar whose amateur interest in music led him to become one of the pioneers of folk-music collecting in Sweden. The achievement of political independence by Norway in 1814 led to an outburst of patriotic feeling in the poetry of Henrik Wergeland (1808–1845), and during the next two decades gave rise to Norwegian schools of painting, poetry, drama and music, and to the study of peasant lore, language, arts and crafts. The

---

[1] Geijer's letters and diaries frequently mention his attempts at composition. His comments on English musical life during his tour in 1809–10 are of considerable interest: for example, he describes one of Samuel Wesley's recitals of Bach and Handel organ works that lasted four hours (*sic*) and was heard with close attention by a large audience; 'a Swedish audience would have begun to cough, chatter, or leave after the first hour'.

Norwegian nationalist movement gave fresh impetus to romantic explorations in Denmark, as despite political separation social and cultural ties between the two countries remained strong.

The collecting of ballads and folk songs, which had begun in Denmark and Sweden as far back as the sixteenth century,[1] was now ardently taken up again. Ludvig Holberg in the eighteenth century had poured contempt upon the ballad as a barbarous diversion for the illiterate, but its status rose with the appearance of 'nordic' collections and imitations in neighbouring countries, such as the *Ossian* forgeries of James Macpherson, the *Reliques of Antient English Poetry* published in 1765 by Thomas Percy, the odes of Friedrich Klopstock (who lived for some time in Copenhagen) and the writings of the French antiquarian, J. H. Mallet. It was under the inspiration of 'Ossian' and Klopstock that Johannes Ewald wrote his Norse plays, *Balders Død* and *Fiskerne*, for which, as we have seen, J. E. Hartmann provided the music.

In the collection and publication of folk music Denmark again led the way, with the five volumes of *Udvalgte Danske Viser fra Middelalderen*, edited by W. H. F. Abrahamson, Rasmus Nyerup, and F. L. Rahbek, and published between 1812 and 1814, with a number of tunes in the last volume. More tunes were included in two volumes edited in 1821 by Nyerup and P. Rasmussen and entitled *Udvalg af danske Viser . . . med Melodier*. The words of Danish ballads had been printed in earlier centuries, but in his 50 *Gamle Kæmpervisemelodier*, published in two volumes (1840 and 1842), C. E. F. Weyse made the traditional ballad-tunes accessible, though modified and harmonized to conform to the taste of the period; and Weyse's pupil and biographer, A. P. Bergreen, dealt similarly with the melodies in his eleven books of *Folkesange og Melodier fædrelandske og fremmede* (1842–1870).

A later generation was to adopt a more realistic and scientific attitude to the preservation of folk-music by going to the living sources. Thus Evald Tang Kristensen (1843–1929), the Cecil Sharp of Denmark,[2] noted down songs directly from the singing

---

[1] See page 31.

[2] See Plate XIX. From 1922 Kristensen had Percy Grainger as a collaborator in his field work. Photostats and reproductions of Grainger's

of the Jutland peasantry and published them under the titles of *Jyske Folkeviser of Toner* (1868) and *Jyske Folkeminder* (1871 onwards). Svend Grundtvig, son of the religious and educational reformer, applied scientific principles to the collection of traditional songs and founded a society for the publication of *Danmarks gamle Folkeviser* from 1853 onwards. Grundtvig also reaped a rich harvest in the Faeroe Islands, and his *Corpus carminum faeroensium* containing about 70,000 stanzas is still in course of publication. To Grundtvig again is due an important collection of Icelandic songs, *Islenzk Fornkvaedi* (1854–1885), which was later supplemented by Bjarne Thorsteinsson's *Islenzk Thjodlög* (1909). Grundtvig's methods had considerable influence on the work of the American scholar, Francis J. Child (1825–1896), author of *English and Scottish Popular Ballads*.

Radical views on the restoration of folk-tunes, in respect of both pitch and rhythm, were advanced by Thomas Linneman Laub (1852–1927), who incidentally composed the pleasing modal clock-chimes one can hear every quarter of an hour from the Copenhagen Town Hall. Laub believed that a close connection existed between mediaeval folksong and Gregorian plainchant, and although his theories are not universally accepted he did much to liberate Danish folk music from the early nineteenth century conventions of rhythm and tonality that Weyse and Bergreen had imposed upon it.

In Norway pioneer work was carried out by the organist Ludvig Mathias Lindeman (1812–1887), the most distinguished member of a famous musical family. Lindeman first contributed a short melodic supplement to Jorgen Moe's collection of Norwegian peasant verses[1] and in the following year brought out a book of 68 *Norske Fjeldmelodier* ('Mountain melodies') with his own admirable harmonizations. In 1848 he received a state subsidy enabling him to travel about Norway and collect songs and instrumental tunes, and the fruits of these journeys appeared in three volumes of *Aeldre og nyere Fjeldmelodier* (1853–1867), which contained nearly six hundred tunes. Lindeman's scholarly but rugged settings, with their lively contrapuntal interest and strong sense of colour, left their mark not only on

Danish collection are in the possession of the British Institute of Recorded Sound.

[1] *Sange, Folkeviser og Stev i Norske Almuedialekter* (1840).

Grieg, Svendsen and other Scandinavian composers but also on the national romantic schools, with their folk-music borrowings or imitations, in other lands. The device of presenting a short repeated or sequential phrase against a constantly changing harmonic background, with free use of chromatic and diatonic dissonances, proved especially helpful in absorbing folk-tunes into larger structures. The following *Springdans*[1] will provide an example of Lindeman's treatment of an instrumental dance tune:

Lindeman's studies in Norwegian folk music were carried further by Catherinus Elling (1858–1943), and with great devotion and depth of scholarship by Dr. O. M. Sandvik

---

[1] *Aeldre og nyere Fjeldmelodier*, Vol. I, no. 143.

(b. 1875).[1] Perhaps the most interesting recent discoveries have been in the field of religious song. L. M. Lindeman's chorale book published in 1877 (revised 1926) superseded that of his father, Ole Andreas Lindeman, who in 1835 had produced the first chorale book to be compiled expressly for Norway. The younger Lindeman and his successors were able to demonstrate that many Lutheran tunes introduced to the Norwegian peasantry in the seventeenth century and later had undergone remarkable changes. In village churches without organs, where the vocal improvisations of parish clerks and the more exuberant members of the congregation could flourish unhindered, imaginative and often impressive variants on the chorales were produced and handed down locally until modern times, when they were recorded by collectors. The following version was obtained in Gloppen, Nordfjord:[2]

(a) Original melody, from the secular song 'Venus du und dein Kind' (see page 37) attributed to Jacob Regnart, and used as a chorale tune in Gesius' *Gesangbuch* (1605) and in Schein's *Cantional* (1627) where it is set to 'Auf meinen lieber Gott'. It was also used in Denmark by Arreboe for his song on the victory of Kalmar: 'O Danmark hør og mærk':

(b) Variant (verbal accents shown by vertical strokes; quarter-tones by crosses):

---

[1] See the long and important article on 'Folk Music (Norwegian)' in *Grove's Dictionary of Music and Musicians* (5th edtn.).

[2] Collected by Dr. O. Ryssdal and printed in *Norsk Musikkgranskning Årbok* 1943–6; quoted by permission of Dr. O. M. Sandvik, whose own *Norske religiøse Folketoner*, Vol. I, Oslo, 1960, contains interesting examples of folk-variants of chorales and psalm-tunes.

The earliest important Swedish collection of folk music, *Svenska folkvisor* (1814–16), was the work of E. G. Geijer and A. A. Afzelius; the former as we have seen was a poet and amateur composer who wrote some sixty songs of his own in a Mozartian style, while Afzelius was primarily an antiquarian.[1] The other standard Swedish collection is that of A. I. Arwidsson (*Svenska fornsånger*, published in three volumes between 1834 and 1842). These early Swedish editors were without the musical standing of Weyse in Denmark, much less the resource and taste of Lindeman in Norway, and perhaps for that reason folk music did not enter as fully into the environment of Swedish composers and educationists as it has in the other two countries. During the nineteenth century Sweden had no Grieg (for Sjögren is not entirely his counterpart) and in the twentieth century none of her most vital and original composers have linked their work with the popular tradition as Carl Nielsen did in Denmark. Nevertheless, a large amount of Swedish folk music is now preserved in archives and publications and serious musicians have directed their attention to the instrumental tunes or *låtar*, which were of comparatively slight interest to the first collectors, with their literary preoccupations.[2]

This brings us to the consideration of some of the instruments traditionally used by the folk musicians of the Scandinavian

---

[1] The Geijer and Afzelius collection was revised in 1830 by Richard Bergström and furnished with a volume of tunes by L. Höijer.

[2] A collection of about 18,000 *Svenska Låtar* was edited by Olof Andersson from 1922 to 1940 on behalf of the Swedish Folk Music Commission.

countries. Lindeman's *Fjeldmelodier* contains many examples of the Norwegian instrumental tunes, and his realization of the melodic and rhythmic individuality of the dance-forms (*gangar*, *springdans*, and *halling*), and also of the striking harmonic implications of the Hardanger fiddle (*hardingfele*) is reflected in the many arrangements and imitations produced by Kjerulf, Grieg, Svendsen, Halvorsen, and later Norwegian composers. The *hardingfele*, a bowed instrument with four upper and four sympathetic lower strings,[1] seems to have developed during the latter part of the Reformation period, perhaps as a branch of the *viola d'amore* family. It reached the peak of its popularity in the eighteenth century, and survived almost into modern times in some of the mountain valleys.

Among the most famous exponents of the *hardingfele* was Torgeir Audunsson, known as *Myllarguten* ('The miller's boy'), who was born in Telemark in 1801, at the age of thirty met the violinist Ole Bull in Bergen, and gave some recitals there under Ole Bull's patronage. A somewhat younger man, Knut Dale (b. 1834) towards the end of his life got into touch with Grieg, at whose suggestion he dictated his repertory of *hardingfele* tunes to Johan Halvorsen. The transcripts made by Halvorsen for the ordinary violin became the basis of Grieg's pianoforte *Slåtter* (op. 72).[2]

During the nineteenth century the *hardingfele* yielded to the normal violin in some districts of Norway (it had never been widespread in Sweden), although it left its influence in the occasional tuning of a fourth (A–D) between the lowest strings.

Survivals of still older stringed instruments remained until recently in Norway, Sweden, Iceland, and Finland. We have already noticed some of the early accounts or representations,

[1] The commonest tuning of the upper strings is A, with the under-strings tuned D–E–Fsharp–A; a favourite alternative is A, with the under-strings tuned C–E–G–A.

[2] One of the *Slåtter* is recorded, both on the *hardingfele* and in Grieg's piano version, in *The History of Music in Sound*, H.M.V., Vol. IX.

and to these we may add two references from authors in the seventeenth century. Corvinus mentions in his *Heptachordum Danicum* (1646) that the *monochordium*—clearly a variety of one-stringed instrument—had been in use among the Danish peasants from antiquity; and a Swedish scholar, G. Stiernhielm, stated in his *De Hyperboreis* (published posthumously in 1685), that one could not enter the poorest cottage without finding there 'Citherum, aut monochordium, aut aliud instrumentum musicum. Omnes fere sunt fidicines.' ('Nearly everybody plays a stringed instrument'.) Stiernhielm seems to be thinking of three types of instrument: a harp or lyre, a plucked or bowed instrument of the *langeleik* family, and perhaps a keyed fiddle or hurdy-gurdy.

Of the three types, the *langeleik* flourished most widely, being found in the nineteenth and early twentieth centuries in Iceland, Norway, and Sweden. In different areas it varied both in nomenclature (*langharpe, langspel, langspil*) but also in number of strings, since although there was only one melody-string there might be several drones.[1] Sometimes it was plucked, sometimes bowed, and in some forms there were movable bridges for stopping the melody string, as in the mediaeval monochord. The plucked *langeleik* was still being played in Valdres in western Norway in the last century, and descendants of it exist as folk-instruments among the Scandinavian communities of North America. In Iceland the *langspil* was always bowed, perhaps under the influence of the two-stringed *fidla*, another late-surviving stringed instrument.

The bowed and keyed fiddle, called in Denmark *noglefejle* and in Sweden *nyckelharpa*, was likewise of mediaeval descent, and had a lengthy life, especially in parts of Sweden; the oldest extant specimen is dated 1526, and they were still being made in a district of Uppland in the late 1920s. The mechanism, with a rotary bow and keys for stopping the strings, is in all essentials that of the mediaeval hurdy-gurdy or *organistrum*.

Wind instruments used among the peasant communities included the willow pipe (*seljeflöyte*); the straight wooden or birch-bark trumpet familiar to tourists in modern Norway

---

[1] Dr. O. M. Sandvik gives the tuning as G for the melody-string and c', g', c", c", e", g" for the drones (article 'Folk-music (Norwegian)' in *Grove's Dictionary*.

(*trælur, langelur, gjætelur*); and the short natural horn (Nor-wegian *bukkehorn*, Swedish *låtpipa*) with finger-holes like the baroque cornett. The following example of a Swedish *hornlåt* is taken from Dybeck's *Folkemelodier* (1853–6):

Reference has already been made to the *kantele*, the national instrument of the Finns, and to its legendary origin.[1] Before closing this chapter it may be of interest to deal briefly with the dawn of the romantic age in Finland, and with the revelation of the unique Finnish folk poetry and music. Curiously enough, one of the earliest glimpses western Europeans gained of that strange world came through an English book, Joseph Acerbi's *Travels through Sweden, Finland and Lapland . . . in the years 1798 and 1799*, published in London in 1802. Acerbi was gifted with acute observation and a lively pen; he also had had a scientific training and was a keen amateur musician. One of the most valuable parts of his work is the collection of Finnish tunes given in the appendix to the second volume, and of great interest also is a plate depicting the 'extraordinary mode of singing by Finlanders'.[2] Acerbi gives a verbal account of the same thing—the chanting in duet form of epic poems such as were later to be incorporated in *Kalevala*—and in another passage he describes the singing and drum-playing of the Lapps. Acerbi found the Finnish towns almost cut off from western music, and he gives an amusing account of how with the help of a fellow-traveller and two local players he was able to let the inhabitants of Uleaborg hear a quartet for the first time.

A generation after Acerbi's visit, the Finnish medical officer Elias Lönnrot published three volumes of folk-poetry under the title of *Kantele* (1831), and four years later he brought out the first edition of *Kalevala*, a composite epic compiled from popular legends handed down from pre-Christian times and versified in the metre most familiar to English and American readers

[1] See Ch. I, p. 17.
[2] See Plate XIII.

XIII 'Extraordinary mode of singing by Finlanders'; from *Acerbi's Travels through Sweden, Finland and Lapland . . . in the years 1798 and 1799*

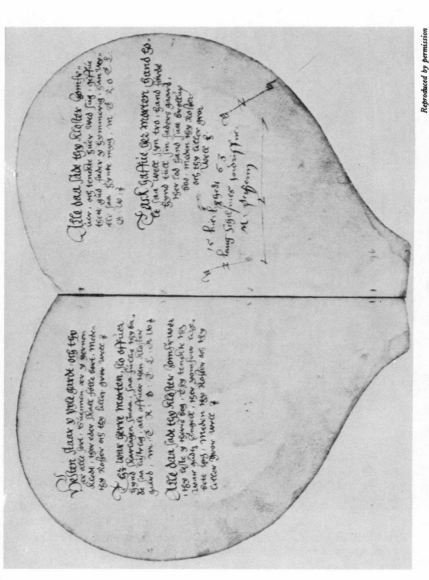

XIV Heart-shaped manuscript book containing Danish ballad-verses, ca. 1553–1555;
Royal Library, Copenhagen

from Longfellow's adoption of it in his *Song of Hiawatha*. Finland now had a double cultural heritage: some of the greatest poets writing in the Swedish language in the eighteenth and early nineteenth century—Creutz, Kellgren, and Runeberg (1804–1877) were Finns, and their verse was henceforward ranged beside the *Kalevala* poems in the totally different Finnish tongue.

One of Runeberg's works, *Fänrik Ståls Sägner* ('Ensign Stål's Tales'), dealing with the Swedish-Russian war and the loss of a large part of Finland to the Russians in 1808, begins with the invocation *Vårt land* ('Our country'), which, set to music by Fredrik Pacius (1809–1891) became one of the national anthems. Pacius, a musician of German origin and a pupil of Spohr, is regarded as the father of Finnish music. As lecturer at the university of Helsingfors he reorganized student music, composed male voice choruses, and began to collect Finnish folk songs, which were known as *kanteletar* after the traditional instrument used for accompanying, the *kantele*. By the end of the nineteenth century the work thus begun by Pacius had grown into the voluminous *Suomen kansan sävelmiä*, edited (1904–1933) by Krohn, Launis and Vaïsanen and containing songs in both the languages of Finland.

7

Lyric Song and Pianoforte Miniature

Although it was not until the beginning of the nineteenth century that the wealth of folk music created by the Scandinavian peasantry began to enter into the lives of the more sophisticated classes, there had come into existence during the past two hundred years a large number of collections of songs and instrumental pieces for the use of cultured amateurs. Some of these songs were secular, like the *Oden und Lieder* of 1642, already referred to; others, of a religious, often pietistic character, were intended to supplement the chorale books for devotional exercises in the home: such were the Norwegian Dorothe Engelbretsdatter's *Sjaelens Sangoffer* (1677) and Petter Dass's *Katekismussange* (1698), the Danish Thomas Kingo's *Aandeligt Sjunge-Kor* (1675), and Hans Adolf Brorson's *Troens rare Klenodie* (1739) and *Svanesangen* (1765). During the romantic period this body of popular urban song-literature was to be cross-fertilized through the serious musician's discovery of peasant song, and thus to give rise to one of the most distinctive forms cultivated by Scandinavian composers, the strophic art-song.

The main link between Danish baroque and rococo song is provided by J. A. P. Schultz (1747–1800), the German-born director of the Copenhagen Royal Theatre from 1787. In his successive song-collections—the significantly titled *Lieder im Volkston* (1782–5) with German texts, *Hellige Sange* (1785) with Danish texts by Edward Horn, and *Viser og Sange* (1792) with German texts translated into Danish, Schultz showed his

98

understanding of the taste and temperament of his adopted country at this period. But his chief contribution to the development of Danish lyric song was made through his best pupil, Christoph Ernst Friedrich Weyse (1774–1842), who also migrated from Germany and made his permanent home in Copenhagen.

It was Weyse's good fortune to live during the golden age of Danish romantic poetry, when the verses of Oehlenschläger, Ingeman, Grundtvig, Heiberg and Winther were coming into being and waiting to be set to music. Weyse also responded to the inspiration of German poets, especially Goethe and Schiller. At his best he can stand comparison with Schubert in his ability to strike from the first bar into the heart of a poem, to fashion a melody so that it sounds completely spontaneous, and to feel the inevitable moment for a modulation or change of colour in the harmony. His piano *ritornelli* are never perfunctory and are often eloquent. His range of style extends from the simplicity of the children's songs (to words by B. S. Ingeman) to the academic elaboration of the cantatas produced for state occasions or the impassioned Weberian arias in *Faruk* (1812) and *Ludlams Hule* (1816), both of which were operatic works to libretti by Oehlenschläger. At times he almost recaptured the spirit of the mediaeval ballad, and in the ambitious opera *Festen paa Kenilworth* he accepted the challenge of Walter Scott's dramatized history in an adaptation by Hans Andersen. In another vein he could turn to a homelier theme and create one of his most successful stage works, *Et Eventyr in Rosenborg Have*, a one-act idyll set in the quiet park behind the Rosenborg castle. The poetry of Heiberg, who was the librettist of the *syngespil* just mentioned, often called forth Weyse's most attractive melodies, as in the short strophic *Barcarole*. (See page 100.)

Weyse had a worthy successor as a song-writer in Peter Heise (1830–1879), who in producing about two hundred songs in the course of his comparatively short life set almost every Danish poet of importance from Oehlenschläger to Emil Aarestrup. During his student days in Leipzig he came into contact with Schumann, and in his own country he mixed freely with men of letters and shared the intellectual excitement of the revolutionary ideals of 1848 and of the Scandinavian literary movement. In his songs he owes much to Weyse, and his earlier

('The night is so still, the air so clear; the dew-pearls tremble, the moonbeams play on the surface of the lake. The melodies of the waves lull the heart, sighing and lamentation cease, the wind's breath sets free the burdened soul.')

works are chiefly in the simple strophic style of the older man. Heise's more mature work shows a deeper insight into romantic poetry, especially when he sets verses by Christian Winther, a writer he greatly admired; his technical range then expands, as in the splendid setting of Winther's *Skovensomhet* ('Solitude in the woods') which is too long to quote here. But generally Heise uses the piano with reticence, subordinating it to the voice-part, in which his gift of spontaneity rivals that of Weyse:

SKJØN ER VAAREN
words by Christian Winther

Ro - sens spœ - de Mund, og som kla - re Sø! - ver-klok-ker klin- ger Fug - le-sang i Lund.

(4 bars) ritornello

('Lovely is the Spring! Delightfully the sun colours the bright foliage of the beech; the woodruff sends out its perfume, and the violet blushingly opens its eye; behind smooth green tresses smiles the tender mouth of the rose, and like clear silver bells rings the bird's song in the grove.')

In Sweden also the poets of the romantic period inspired a circle of song-writers. One of the earliest composers to set the verses of Tegnér was Bernhard Crusell (1775–1838), a Finnish bandmaster who also wrote some admirable clarinet concertos. But the title of 'the Swedish Schubert' has sometimes been awarded to A. F. Lindblad (1801–1876), many of whose two hundred or more songs were in the repertory of Jenny Lind. In his younger days Lindblad belonged to Geijer's literary coterie in Uppsala, and many of his songs are settings of his own verses. He was an enthusiast for the music of Beethoven and Mendelssohn, and emulated them in his instrumental music; but whereas even his C major symphony, warmly praised by Schumann, has been forgotten, his songs endure, and Julius Rabe has called one of them, *En sommardag*, 'the loveliest melody in Swedish music'.

Two other song-writers of the Geijer group must be mentioned briefly. The career of J. A. Josephson (1818–1880) has many points of similarity with Lindblad's; he too was a friend of Jenny Lind, who helped him with funds to study in Germany, and he too was at home in the salons of Uppsala, where from the middle of the century he was regarded as the country's leading professional musician. In his song-writing he tends towards a richer texture than Lindblad, showing the influence of Schumann's piano style in the *Lieder*. A curious member of the same group was C. J. L. Almqvist (1793–1866), a prolific man of letters who tried to discover by experiment how far an amateur composer could go without technical training. As a poet he was considered the most original of the Geijer circle. He writes in a dream-world (he used the French title *Songes* for some of his poems) allows prose to glide into verse and verse into song, at which point a melody of the author's own composition is interpolated. Almqvist also wrote down some thirty 'free fantasies' for piano. The contemporary composer and critic, Moses Pergament, appears to think highly of Almqvist's talent[1], and has arranged some of his pieces in two orchestral suites under the title of *Almqvistiana*.

Although the name of Emil Sjögren (1853–1918) was formerly associated chiefly with effective drawing-room piano pieces and sonatas for strings and piano, his reputation in Sweden rests now chiefly on his songs, of which he wrote nearly a hundred. His first published work was a set of four songs to poems by Bjørnson (1876), and his sympathy with Norwegian literature and his admiration for Grieg always gave a Norwegian tinge to his style. He also drew upon the Danish and German romantic poets, and his songs from Heyse and Geibel's *Spanisches Liederbuch* were written some years before Hugo Wolf's settings. Unlike most Scandinavian song-writers, Sjögren made comparatively little use of strophic form; many of his finest songs are *durchkomponierte*, with a rich and imaginative use of the piano, and are too long to quote in full. The following short extract is from a setting of one of the Danish poet Holger Drachmann's *Tannhäuser* songs:

[1] Pergament, M., *C. J. L. Almqvist, den geniale amatören* (*Svenska Tonsättare*), Stockholm, 1943.

('And I will pluck the flowers of the South, but will not take their thorns too.')

Reproduced by permission of Carl Gehrmans Förlag, Copenhagen.

Following upon the re-emergence of Norway as an independent nation (though still at that time loosely allied to Sweden) in 1814, a national literature took its origin in the poets Wergeland and Welhaven, and reached its first climax in the dramatists Bjørnstjerne Bjørnson (1832–1910) and Henrik Ibsen (1828–1906), both of whom represent not only the culmination of the national romantic movement but also the reaction against it and the beginnings of modern realism. Parallel developments took place in the other arts. A school of national painters, Dahl, Tidemand and Gude, returned from their travels in 1849, at almost the same time as the violinist Ole Bull settled in his native country after half a lifetime of adventure in the old and new worlds. In music a characteristic Norwegian idiom asserted itself before Grieg adopted it and made it his own. Its creation was mainly the work of three Norwegians—L. M. Lindeman, Rikaard Nordraak, and Halfdan Kjerulf.[1]

[1] Touches of Norwegian colouring, probably derived from folk-dance rhythms and melodic progressions, can be found in the piano pieces of Thomas Dyke Ackland Tellefsen (1823–74), a pupil and friend of Chopin. For a full critical study of Tellefsen with musical examples, see *Norsk*

Lindeman's contribution through his great collection of folk music, and still more through his manner of harmonizing folk-tunes, has already been described. It is worth remembering also that he was a first-class executant, that he was one of the organists invited to give the opening recitals on the new Albert Hall organ in 1871, and that the foundation of his organ school in Christiania in 1883 gave the Norwegian capital the foundations of its present Conservatory. In complete contrast, Rikaard Nordraak was little more than a dilettante whose influence on Norwegian music was out of proportion to his innate musical talent. He died of consumption in 1866 in his twenty-fourth year, leaving a few songs for solo voice and for male voice choir, among them the setting of his cousin Bjørnson's national hymn, *Ja, vi elsker dette Landet* ('Yes, we love this country'), and fragments of incidental music to some of Bjørnson's plays. The songs contain, especially in their *ritornelli*, many touches of melody and harmony that suggest the idiom of Grieg, but are in reality derived from Norwegian folk song and dance as recorded and arranged by Lindeman and his imitators. A typical example is Nordraak's setting, written in 1859, of *Treet*, a lyric from Bjørnson's 'folk-novel' *Arne*, in the closing bars of which we have several 'Norse' ingredients—the pedal point, the sequences, the sharpened fourth of the scale, the fall from tonic to dominant via the leading-note, and the feminine cadence:

Musikkgranskning Årbok 1956–8, article by H. Huldt-Nystrøm. pp. 80–198. Passages in the Andante of the *Sonata for Two Pianos* (Op. 41) are particularly interesting for their Norse flavour.

But it was not Nordraak's compositions so much as his infectious enthusiasm for all things Scandinavian that made the strongest impression on his contemporaries—his conversation and letter-writing and his activity in the society known as 'Euterpe' which he had formed, with Edvard Grieg, Emil Horneman, and G. Matthison-Hansen, as a progressive rival to the well-established 'Musikforeningen' in Copenhagen. Nordraak was the catalytic agent that brought about the transmutation of Grieg from a disciple of the Leipzig school into an ardent nationalist whose finest work was to be achieved mainly in the strophic song and the keyboard miniature or song without words.

Before discussing Grieg's work in these fields, however, a few words are due to the third member of the trio of Grieg's predecessors. Halfdan Kjerulf's personality was less vivid than Nordraak's, and his influence was less obvious. A link between the two is their devotion to the poetry of Bjørnson, which invariably raises the temperature of Kjerulf's shy talent and sometimes evokes from him settings hardly inferior to the best of Grieg; examples can be found in the Bjørnson songs, *Prinsessen*, *Ung Venevil*, and the song from *Synnøve Solbakken* with its hummed introduction that may have suggested the familiar instrumental prelude to Solveig's song in Grieg's music to *Peer Gynt*. Kjerulf was not an ardent nationalist like Ole Bull or Nordraak, though he could arrange a folk-tune with devotion and good taste. His sympathies were rather with the conservative Scandinavianism of Welhaven, a poet whose verses he liked to set. His piano pieces, like the songs, are slight in texture and restrained in emotional expression; technically they derive from Mendelssohn, but are seldom without a touch of individuality. As a teacher of the piano he had considerable success, and could claim both Erika Lie and Agathe Backer-Gröndahl as his pupils.[1]

Despite the immense popularity of his instrumental work, it is generally agreed that Edvard Hagerup Grieg (1843–1907) excelled as a song-writer. Indeed, the whole course of his development as a composer can be traced through his songs. Some of his earliest publications were settings of German poems

[1] See *Norsk Musikkgranskning Årbok* 1959–61 for a study of Kjerulf's piano music, by Nils Grinde.

by Heine and Chamisso, and were written while he was still a student at Leipzig. Soon after, in 1864, came his betrothal to his cousin Nina Hagerup and his meeting with Hans Andersen, some of whose Danish poems Grieg chose for his op. 5 collection *Hjertets Melodier* and also for most of the op. 18 set of *Romanser*. With the four songs from Bjørnson's *Fiskerjenten* ('The fisher-lass'), published in 1870 as op. 21, Grieg appears as the legitimate successor to Kjerulf in his response to Bjørnson's virile and sensitive verse. Grieg's most extended song, *Fra Monte Pincio*, belongs to the same period and also has a text by Bjørnson. A few years later Grieg turned to the other giant of Norwegian literature, Henrik Ibsen, six of whose poems he set as op. 25; this was in 1876, and in the same year he produced the set of five songs to words by another Norwegian poet, John Paulsen (op. 26).

In the following year Grieg's song-writing entered upon a fresh phase, with the beginning of his interest in the *landsmaal* or dialect verses of A. O. Vinje, the philologist who laid the foundations of modern Norwegian (*Nynorsk*) as a language distinct from Danish, and whose nostalgic poetry has something in common with that of A. E. Housman. Grieg's Vinje songs, written at great speed, were eventually published as the *Melodier* of op. 33. Another manifestation of Grieg's increasing love for pure Norse poetry was his setting of the ballad *Den Bergtekne* for baritone solo, strings and horns (op. 32). The Children's Songs (op. 61) written in 1894–5 are charming miniatures and among the best music ever composed for children to sing. In 1896–8 Grieg wrote what are perhaps his most eloquent songs, again to *landsmaal* verses, this time the lyric poems introduced into Arne Garborg's story *Haugtussa* (op. 67).

Only within fairly recent times, and partly through broadcasting and the gramophone, have Grieg's Scandinavian songs become known abroad in their original languages—Danish and the two forms of Norwegian. In the past clumsy German translations have done the composer poor service, not only because of the false declamation they impose on the singer, and the actual mistranslations with which they baffle the hearer, but also on account of the erroneous use of the term *Lieder* which goes with the German versions. Grieg's songs are not *Lieder* but *Romanser*, in the tradition of other Scandinavian songs of the romantic period, including those of Weyse, Heise, Kjerulf, and to a more limited extent Sjögren. The composer of *Romanser* relies on the poem and the interpreter to communicate subtle variations in rhythm and mood from stanza to stanza, against a musical background that remains constant, with little organic development and with the piano accompaniment subordinated to the declamation of the poem. No better example could be cited than the opening of *Vaaren* ('The Spring'), from the Vinje songs (op. 33, no. 2), where flexibility in the voice part is combined with an accompaniment whose lay-out is calculated to give support and create atmosphere by the simplest means, but to stand the many repetitions needed when the song is sung complete.

Grieg's numerous short piano pieces are so closely akin to the songs that it is not surprising to find that they follow a similar course of progression through a German, a Danish and a Norwegian phase. The German influence soon waned, that of the Danish romantics Gade and J. P. E. Hartmann lasted longer;[1] the turning-point was Grieg's meeting with Nordraak in 1864, and his course was finally determined by the discovery of Lindeman's *Fjeldmelodier* in 1869. His own first attempts at arranging folk-tunes for the piano in his op. 17 (1870) follow Lindeman's methods; but only when Grieg had been able to hear folk songs and fiddle tunes at first hand was he able to integrate living Norwegian folk music with his personal style in the *Norske Folkeviser* of 1896 (op. 66), the remarkable *Slåtter* of 1902 (op. 72)—arranged, as we have already seen, from Halvorsen's transcriptions of Knut Dale's traditional *hardingfele* playing, and some of the most original of the Lyric Pieces, like *Klokkeklang* (op. 54, no. 6), and *Aften på Höjfeldet* (op. 68, no. 4) —two impressionist sketches, the one of bell-ringing heard from a distant spire and the other of an evening scene in the mountains. It was this *nouveau Grieg* that excited so much interest among Parisian musicians about the turn of the century.[2]

---

[1] If Grieg has a counterpart among Danish late romantics, it is Peter Erasmus Lange-Müller (1850–1926), whose mildly impressionistic piano pieces, nostalgic songs, and incidental music to Drachmann's play *Der var engang* . . . occupy a place in the affections of his countrymen.

[2] For a full study of Grieg's music, with a bibliography, see *Grieg: a Symposium*, edtd. Gerald Abraham, London, 1948.

Space must be found here to mention a talented contemporary of Grieg's, the concert pianist and composer Agathe
Backer-Gröndahl. She was a pupil of Lindeman and Kjerulf
and also studied at Leipzig. Her piano pieces and songs are
fertile in ideas, and show a command of technique that allows
her to express warmth of romantic feeling without senti-
mentality. Her settings of poems by Vilhelm Krag are particularly fine in their bold phrasing and sonorous piano-writing:

('All the world shall sing thy bridal day, and the heath on
the hillside shall glow, and the light shall heave in mighty
waves, and the wind ride in youth's wild chase over every
sunlit mountain.')

The works of this remarkable woman deserve to be more widely
known and sung outside her native country.

Among Finnish song-writers of the period the most prominent

are Crusell and Pacius, who have already been mentioned;
Martin Wegelius (1846–1906), the first director of the Helsing-
fors conservatory opened in 1882, and one of the teachers of
Sibelius; Richard Frederik Faltin (1835–1918), who succeeded
Pacius at the university, and Robert Kajanus (1856–1935). As
most of these musicians were trained in Germany, and had no
close contacts with the stronger nationalist elements in western
Scandinavia, their settings of Swedish verse lack much of the
colour of the Swedish and Norwegian romantic song-composers.
More interest attaches to their experiments in handling the
Finnish language, with its individual rhythmic and grammatical
structure, and here can be found the beginnings of a national
idiom in Finnish music. In the following excerpt from a
Qwarnsång ('Mill-song') by Pacius the language is Swedish, but
the melody is based on purely Finnish folk-tune with its
quintuple *Kalevala* metre:

('Once I was rosy-cheeked, and swayed like a rose before the
wind.')

The work of these earlier Finnish composers was to have
important bearings on that of Jean Sibelius, and especially on
his song-writing.

8

Orchestral and Chamber Music in the Nineteenth Century

Wе have already seen that instrumental music flourished in Denmark and Sweden in the seventeenth century, and that the greater churches made use of a variety of instruments to supplement their imposing organs. By 1773 Abraham Hülphers[1] was able to record that nearly five hundred organs existed in the churches of Sweden alone. In the larger centres of population both professional and amateur orchestral playing developed during the eighteenth century,[2] but especially in Stockholm where the enthusiasm of J. H. Roman exerted its greatest influence and where men of high social rank did not disdain to take part. Thus Claes

[1] Hülphers, A., *Historisk Afhandling om Musik och Instrumenter . . . jämte beskrifning öfver orgverken in Sverige*, Västeras, 1773.

[2] Turku, the seat of the Finnish University from 1640 until 1827, was an important centre of amateur and semi-professional music which founded its own Musical Society in 1790, with a large library of scores and parts. In Norway, the Bergen Musical Society *Harmonien* was founded as early as 1765, and can claim to be the oldest institution of its kind surviving in Scandinavia, and one of the oldest in Europe; its name is still borne by Bergen's symphony orchestra, now entirely professional. Among the founder-members of *Harmonien* was John Grieg, grandfather of the composer, and Ole Bull was admitted as a performing member at the age of nine. The Trondhjem Musical Society dates from 1786; among its founders were J. H. Berlin (see below, p. 113) and the seventeen-year-old O. A. Lindeman. The state of instrumental music in Christiania in 1815, with proposals for founding and equipping an academy, is described in a pamphlet by L. Noverud, *Et Blick paa Musikens Tilstand i Norge*, reprinted in facsimile by the Oslo University Press, 1957.

Ekeblad, the Swedish Lord High Steward, relates in his diary in December 1762 (a few years after Roman's death) how he has himself been playing in the orchestra at a charity concert organized by the Freemasons, and found that the orchestra 'n'était composé que de fraymaçons et de personnes de la plus haute volée.'

Much string music by contemporary Italian composers like Locatelli, Sarti, Galuppi, and Jomelli found its way into Sweden, and native composers imitated its style. The leading Swedish violinist of the period, Anders Wesström, (1722–1781), who had been a pupil of Tartini, composed four quintets in the manner of Boccherini, two sextets for string and horns, sonatas for violin and for 'cello, two overtures and two symphonies. Ferdinand Zellbell (1689–1765), an outstanding organist and theorist who succeeded Roman as court music director, and his son, also named Ferdinand Zellbell (1710–1780), spanned the gap between the death of Roman and the appearance of Berwald; they wrote music for state occasions and organized a series of 'cavalier concerts' with an orchestra of about fifty amateurs, like the one described by Ekeblad.

Two pupils, or disciples, of Roman were Per Brant (1713–1767), two of whose symphonies survive, and Johan Miklin (d. 1750), whose son of the same name succeeded him as 'Director Musices' at Linköping and wrote treatises on organ-building and thorough-bass. But the most prominent composer in Sweden at this time was Joseph Martin Kraus (1756–1792), who came from Germany in 1778,[1] and whose important operatic work left him time to write four symphonies, nine string quartets, and sonatas for violin and for other instruments, the majority of these being among the manuscripts in the Uppsala library. Kraus has been called the Swedish Mozart. Two of his pupils were the organist Johan Wikmanson (1752–1800), who dedicated some of his string quartets to Haydn, and the talented but unbalanced Gustaf Fredrici (1770–1801)

---

[1] Kraus spent some years at the court of Gustaf III, and it was a Swedish court official, Fredrik Samuel Silverstolpe, who in 1797 introduced Haydn to some of the chamber music of Kraus. Haydn already knew of Kraus as a symphonist, and spoke well of him. The orchestral and chamber music of this long-neglected composer is now being published in a modern edition (Nagel-Novello).

Etwas Neues unter der Sonnen!

oder

Das Unterirrdische

Klippen=Concert

in Norwegen/

aus glaubwürdigen Urkunden

auf Begehren angezeiget,

von

Mattheson.

Felsenlied unsichtbarer Geschöpffe.

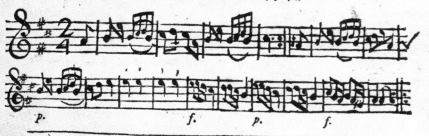

p.   f.   p.   f.

HAMBURG, im Brachmonath, 1740.

Gedruckt bey seel. Thomas von Wierings Erben, im güldnen A. B. C.

Auctor sil sueua in General Major Bertheller, Comandant i Christiana

XV *Das Unterirrdische Klippen-Concert in Norwegen;* title page of pamphlet by Mattheson, 1740

XVI Title-page of song-book by Samuel Simon Weise, published in Copenhagen, 1753; Royal Library, Copenhagen. The background shows a contemporary panorama of the Danish capital.

who studied with Mozart in Vienna, and whose D minor symphony and clarinet quintet have been reconstructed from short-score transcripts, the original full-scores having been destroyed by the composer in a fit of despair. The sole Norwegian representative of the Mannheim School was Johan Henrich Berlin (1741–1808), organist of Trondhjem Cathedral, one of the founders of the Musical Society, and a prolific composer of orchestral and chamber works.[1]

The most gifted Scandinavian composer of instrumental music during the first half of the nineteenth century was the Swedish symphonist Franz Berwald, of whom it has been aptly said that his works 'struck an unromantic and unsentimental note in a romantic age'. Though little appreciated in his own country in his lifetime (1796–1868) Berwald is now acknowledged as one of the founders of modern Swedish music, and even internationally now holds a place of honour among the few symphonists between Beethoven and Brahms whose works are remembered and performed. As with Borodin, service to more than one profession restricted his musical output, and what he managed to write in the midst of other avocations—the invention of orthopaedic appliances, the management of a clinic, directing a glass-blowing factory and a sawmill—was uneven in quality. But at his best he has a clarity and a freshness that are as exhilarating as a northern summer.[2]

Berwald's fame rests chiefly on three of his symphonies, a couple of overtures, and some chamber music. His strong and original personality appears not only in his experiments in form, like the amalgamation of slow movement and scherzo in the *Septet* and the *Sinfonie singulière*, but also in the charm and wit of his musical language, which owes something to Beethoven and not a little to Spohr. His melodic patterns are extremely varied in construction, sometimes keeping mainly to stepwise motion, at others springing and soaring through wide diatonic intervals, as at the opening of the scherzo of the piano quintet:

---

[1] A full biographical and critical account of the Berlin family and their background in eighteenth-century Trondhjem will be found in Dahlback, K., *Rokokkomusikk i trøndersk miljø, Johan Henrich Berlin* (1741–1807). *Norsk Musikkgranskning Årbok* 1954–5.

[2] The standard biographical and critical study is Layton, Robert: *Franz Berwald*, London, 1959.

Berwald's paragraphs may often be built up from short motives organized sequentially; but he is also capable of an unbroken melodic line, like the dozen bars that begin the duo for violin and piano:

In harmony he is often remarkably bold and original. The opening of the *Sinfonie singulière*, with its ascending sequence of fourths over a gradually descending diatonic scale, is prophetic of twentieth-century neo-classical idioms; the sequence of diatonic sevenths in the scherzo of the E flat symphony would not seem out of place in a Debussy prelude; and while some of his most memorable passages are based on diatonic harmony, there are moments when, as in the finale of the quartet for wind and piano, Berwald breaks into chromatic harmony that anticipates Chopin, who was only nine years old in 1819 when Berwald wrote his quartet:

Berwald stood apart from his Scandinavian contemporaries in contributing little to lyric song, but he composed operas, including *Estrella di Soria* and *The Queen of Golconda*, and several cantatas written during the period of intense national feeling round about 1848, on such subjects as Karl XII's victory at Narva, Gustavus Adolphus' victory and death at Lützen, and Gustav Vasa's journey to Dalarna. He was, however, essentially an instrumental composer who, like Berlioz, thought naturally in orchestral sonorities; his piano-writing is often awkward and ineffective, but his orchestral scoring has a translucence and a brilliancy resulting partly from the nature of his part-writing and harmonic syntax, partly from his economical use of instrumental sounds. Passages of pure string writing occur with refreshing frequency, and among the other instruments the timpani are treated with uncommon sensitivity and understanding. The same sense of instrumental values is apparent in his considerable output of chamber music.

Between 1829 and 1842 Berwald spent much of his life in Germany and Austria, and even after settling again in his native Sweden continued to visit the German-speaking countries where much of his best work had been achieved, both in music and in muscular therapy, and where he could count on better-informed criticism than in the provincial artistic climate of Stockholm in the middle of the nineteenth century. His individuality was strong enough, however, to resist the ever-encroaching influence of the German romantics on composers of Scandinavian origin, more and more of whom were making their way to Berlin or Leipzig to study with teachers who tended to reproduce in every country an international romantic (or classical-romantic) style occasionally varied with tints derived from folk music. Typical Swedish products of this school were Albert Rubenson (1826–1901) and Fredrik Vilhelm Ludvig Norman (1831–1885), both of whom studied in Leipzig and there came into contact with Niels Gade. Rubenson wrote a symphony, some chamber music, and incidental music to plays by Hostrup and Bjørnson, all in an idiom that is basically Schumann's with mild Scandinavian colouring. Norman was one of the few Swedish musicians of his time who recognized Berwald's talent, and like Berwald he worked chiefly in the classical forms of the symphony and the string quartet. Two pupils of Berwald followed their master in writing mainly for instruments. They were Joseph Dente (1835–1905), a violinist who produced a symphony in D minor, a violin concerto, and a concert overture; and Jakob Adolf Hägg (1850–1928) who studied with both Berwald and Gade and wrote a *Nordic* symphony and sonatas for piano and 'cello and piano. Another member of Berwald's circle, Oscar Byström is remembered for his C minor string quartet (1856) and for a symphony (1870–2) strongly influenced by Berwald's style.

A Danish contemporary of Berwald is remembered with some gratitude for his contributions to educational piano music and to the repertory of the flute. Friedrich Daniel Rudolph Kuhlau (1786–1832), whose *syngespil*, *Elverhøj*, has already been discussed, migrated from Germany to settle in Copenhagen as a

XVII Opera-production in the Gustavian era; scene from Piccini's *Atys*,
from a painting by Pehr Hilleström of about 1785

XVIII   Musical evening in the house of Christian Waagepeterson, showing Niels Gade at the piano; from the painting by W. N. Marstrand, 1834 : Frederiksborg Castle

young man, and soon became one of the leading pianists and teachers in Denmark. His piano sonatinas were for many generations indispensable to the beginner on the piano, and still have their admirers, and flautists value his many compositions for the flute, both solo and in almost every conceivable combination. Kuhlau was highly respected not only in Denmark, where he received the honorific styles of 'Kammermusikus' and 'Professor', but also in Germany. He was one of the few people who could meet Beethoven on terms of easy friendship, and it is said that they once spent a convivial evening exchanging canons, a form of learned diversion in which Kuhlau excelled.

The first Danish symphony of the romantic period has been ascribed to Johan Peter Emilius Hartmann (1805–1900), grandson of the J. E. Hartmann who collaborated with Ewald in *Fiskerne*. J. P. E. Hartmann's symphony in G minor (1835) won the praises of Spohr and Marschner, and Schumann devoted a series of articles to his works, including the D minor piano sonata with its virile opening. (See page 118.)

Much of Hartmann's long life was occupied in the composition of opera and ballet, and a further account of his work must therefore be left to the next chapter. He outlived his son, Wilhelm Emilius Hartmann (1836–1898), composer of a symphonic poem, *Haakon Jarl*, of three concertos, and of seven symphonies.

The leadership of Danish music during the second half of the nineteenth century was shared between the Hartmanns and Niels Wilhelm Gade (1817–1890), the son of a Copenhagen instrument-maker. Gade studied composition under A. P. Bergreen, and at the age of twenty-four won a prize offered by the newly-formed Copenhagen Music Society (Musikforeningen) with his concert overture *Nachklänge von Ossian* ('Echoes of Ossian'), obviously intended to emulate the success of Mendelssohn's *Fingal's Cave*. A further award, this time from state funds, was gained for a first symphony in C minor, enabling Gade to go to Leipzig for further study, and it was at a Gewandhaus concert, in March 1843, that he heard his symphony performed for the first time under the baton of Mendelssohn. Gade's status at the Leipzig conservatory did not long remain that of a student; he became one of its earliest

professors, and after deputizing for Mendelssohn he took complete charge of the Gewandhaus concerts for a year after Mendelssohn's death in 1847. In the meantime, he had composed his second (E major) and third (A minor) symphonies, and a string octet modelled upon Mendelssohn's youthful masterpiece in that form.

From 1850, when Gade returned to Copenhagen to succeed F. J. Glaeser as conductor of Musikforeningen, his energies were divided between composition and the duties attached to a variety of key posts in the musical life of the capital. He played the organ in some of the larger churches, he was one of the directors of the Conservatory opened in 1866, for a short period he took charge of opera at the Royal Theatre, and as a conductor he did valuable pioneer work by introducing Danish audiences to the *St. Matthew Passion* and Beethoven's ninth symphony, and also contemporary music by Berlioz, Liszt, Wagner and Brahms. He brought the number of his own symphonies to eight and of his overtures to seven, with a multitude of chamber works, piano pieces, and choral compositions. But like Mendelssohn he seldom recaptured the spontaneity and vitality of his earlier years, and the quantity of commissioned writing that came his way increased a natural tendency towards academic dryness. His many cantatas and oratorios written to order for national occasions or for festivals abroad (including the English choral festivals) are mostly forgotten; an exception is the cantata *Elverskud* ('The erl-king's daughter'), composed in 1853, which still retains its popularity with Danish amateur societies and is occasionally revived in England. It contains some of the most beautiful orchestral writing of the romantic period in any country, as in the introduction to the forest scene at night:

Gade's symphonies also were at one time not unfamiliar to English orchestras, but even in Denmark they are now seldom heard and not one appears to have been recorded completely. Like so much of Gade's work they take both form and atmosphere from Mendelssohn, whose A minor *Scottish* symphony is the prototype of many a 'nordic' work. The Danish critic, Charles Kjerulf, however, considered that Gade's fourth symphony in B flat represented a new stage in his development after his return from Germany, and wrote of Gade 'rising phoenix-like from the ashes of his Mendelssohnian past'. The sixth symphony in G minor is still in the repertory of Danish orchestras, and other works deserve re-exploration. The two middle movements of the third symphony in A minor, for example, are scored with delicacy and imagination; such a passage as the following has much of the charm of Dvořák's lighter symphonic movements:

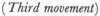

(*Third movement*)

Niels Gade lived at the same time as two other great Danish artists, the writer Hans Christian Andersen and the sculptor Thorwaldsen, and he may perhaps be said to occupy a position midway between them. From time to time he enters into Andersen's dream-world, as in *Elverskud* and some of the shorter piano pieces; but in general he shares Thorwaldsen's reverence for classical forms seen in the light of a restrained romantic imagination. Apart from *Elverskud*, the *Ossian* overture, and a few symphonic movements like the one illustrated above, the best of his work is to be found in the keyboard pieces and in the chamber music. The early violin sonata in A (op. 6), for example, is worthy of attention, if only for the elusive tonality, delicate figuration, and skilful lay-out of violin and piano parts in the opening bars; while the piano sonata (op. 28) is interesting not only for its own robust qualities but also for the obvious influence it exerted on Grieg's piano sonata in the same key (E minor), written in 1865.

To the young Grieg, starting out upon his career, Gade was the embodiment both of the Leipzig tradition and of Scandinavian romantic ideals; and it was in deference to Gade (upon whose name, incidentally, Grieg wrote a fugue in his student days) that Grieg embarked upon a symphony that was never completed but remains as two isolated pieces in a piano duet version. The ambition to conquer the problems of large-scale structure remained with Grieg throughout his life, though he came more and more to realize that his true medium of expression was the strophic song and the piano mood-picture. The works in sonata form—three for violin and piano, one for 'cello and piano, and one, already mentioned, for piano alone, all attempt, with varying success, to superimpose impressionistic colour on stylized outlines of classical form, and the same is true of the concert overture *I Høst* ('In Autumn'), which also was written in emulation of Gade and Mendelssohn. On the other hand, the A minor concerto for piano and orchestra manages to achieve so happy a balance between Scandinavian traditional song and dance idioms and formal considerations that not even the many structural parallels with Schumann's piano concerto detract from its originality and effectiveness. Grieg's only completed string quartet (op. 27, composed in 1877–8) experiments more freely with structure, and in more than one way influenced Debussy's single work for this medium. The remainder of Grieg's large-scale instrumental compositions adopt other methods; the suite *Fra Holbergs Tid*, written for piano in 1884 and arranged for strings in the following year, evokes the atmosphere of Holberg's plays in a pasticcio of eighteenth-century dance measures, and in the *Ballade* (op. 24) for solo piano and the *Old Norwegian Melody* (op. 51) for two pianos, he uses traditional tunes as a basis for concert pieces in variation form.[1]

A Norwegian composer who might, under more favourable conditions have become a true symphonist was Johan Severin Svendsen (1840–1911), whose D major symphony was played in Christiania in 1867, soon after Svendsen's return from his studies in Leipzig, and whose second symphony in B flat is still heard occasionally. Though welcomed in Germany, where he gained the friendship of Liszt and Wagner, and in Denmark, where he finally settled as conductor at the Royal Theatre, he never found the recognition due to his talents in his own land. He retained an affection, however, for Norwegian folk music and wrote five rhapsodies on tunes from Lindeman's collection; his picturesque *Norwegian Artists' Carnival* and orchestral legend *Zorehayda* also testify to his vivid sense of orchestral colour, in which respect he was better endowed than Grieg. As an orchestral conductor he made a lasting impression on standards of performance and taste in Copenhagen, and the help he gave Carl Nielsen in bringing his works before the public makes Svendsen an important figure in the development of modern Scandinavian music. One of Svendsen's pupils, Valdemar Fini Henriques (1867–1940), gained an international reputation as a concert violinist and composer of *salon* music.

While Norway thus lost Svendsen to Denmark, another gifted conductor and composer forsook his native Denmark for the United States. This was Asger Hamerik (1843–1923), brother of the musicologist Angul Hammerich and uncle of the composer Ebba Hamerik (1898–1948). Asger Hamerik spent the most active years of his life as director of the Peabody Institute in Baltimore, which involved conducting a symphony orchestra, and the sixth of his seven symphonies, the well-known *Sinfonie spirituelle*, was written for strings alone on the occasion of a strike in the wind departments. Hamerik also wrote five suites based on Scandinavian folk-tunes.

[1] For a full discussion of the various aspects of Grieg's work, and detailed bibliography, see *Grieg: a Symposium*, edtd. Gerald Abraham, London, 1948. For an outline of the composer's life Horton, J., *Grieg*, London, 1950, may be consulted. The definitive biography is by David Monrad Johansen: *Edvard Grieg*, Oslo, 1934; English translation by M. Robertson, Princeton, 1938. Monrad Johansen is himself a composer of standing.

Another able technician of the orchestra was Johan Halvorsen (1864–1935), a Norwegian violinist who graduated to conducting posts in Bergen and Christiania. He too made effective use of folk-tunes, imitating the fiddle dance-music or *slåtter* he had helped Grieg to collect and write down, and he also produced some effective scores for the theatre.

Although Christian Sinding (1856–1941) became the acknowledged leader of Norwegian music after Grieg's death his work was cosmopolitan in idiom and seldom made use of national colour. He had strong sympathies with Germany, where his fluent and highly professional compositions were admired. Neither his orchestral works—he wrote three symphonies, a piano concerto, and three violin concertos—nor his songs are much performed nowadays, and even his chamber music and once very popular piano pieces have fallen out of fashion in the astringent climate of post-war Scandinavian musical life. Nevertheless, Sinding had the reputation, during the eighteen-eighties, of being an advanced composer, and certain harmonic progressions in his piano quintet (op. 5) attracted hostile criticism.

9

Ballet, Opera, and other Music
for the Stage

The happy relationship that had existed between literature and music in the earlier years of the Scandinavian romantic period continued unbroken throughout the nineteenth century. Hans Andersen in Denmark, Bjørnson and Ibsen in Norway, Strindberg in Sweden, Runeberg and Topelius in Finland all looked to contemporary composers for incidental music to plays and for settings of cantatas, melodramas, and opera texts. The plentiful harvest of Scandinavian lyric song was due, as already noticed, to this fruitful partnership of the arts; and a further development took the form of a distinctive type of ballet in Denmark, and to some extent in Sweden also, making use of Norse legendary subjects mimed to elaborate orchestral scores.

The originator of this unique kind of entertainment was the ballet-master Bournonville, who has some claim to be regarded as the Diaghilev of his time.[1] He enlisted the services of the most eminent composers in Denmark, namely J. P. E. Hartmann and his son-in-law Niels Gade, who collaborated in a score for Bournonville's ballet *Et Folkesaga*, Gade writing the first and third acts and Hartmann the second. It was the older man who found the medium the more congenial, and soon Hartmann, organist of Vor Frue Kirke and holder of various other leading appointments, was producing full-length ballet scores on subjects like *Valkyrien* (1861) and *Thrymskviden* (1868), taken

[1] Fog, Dan: *The Royal Danish Ballet, 1760–1958 and August Bournonville*, Copenhagen, 1961.

XIX Evald Tang Kristensen (1843–1929), Danish folksong collector; from the painting by Hans Agersnap in the National Historical Museum, Frederiksborg Castle

XX Group of modern Hardanger fiddle-players

from Norse mythology. His choral work, *Vølvens Spaadom* ('The witch's prophecy') (1872), belongs to the same legendary world, as do his scores for Oehlenschläger's dramas *Olaf den Hellige* (1838) and *Haakon Jarl* (1854). Hartmann collaborated with other poets also: with J. L. Heiberg in *Syvsoverdag* ('Seven sleepers' day'), written for the coronation festivities of Christian VIII, and with Hans Andersen in *Liden Kirsten* (1846), which is steeped in the atmosphere of the mediaeval ballad as seen through the eyes of the romantic poets, with the refrain of the ballad *Lave og Jon* recurring as a kind of *Leitmotif*.

To his contemporaries, Hartmann's stage music seemed apt, vivid, and exciting. The English literary critic Edmund Gosse wrote enthusiastically of the Bournonville-Hartmann ballets in the eighteen-eighties:[1]

'No visitor to Copenhagen should miss the opportunity of seeing one of these beautiful pieces, the best of all, perhaps, being *Thrymskviden* . . . to which Hartmann has set the wildest, most magical music conceivable . . . the vigour and liveliness of the scenes, the grace and originality of the dances, surprise and delight one to the highest degree.'

Unfortunately the element of surprise is what Hartmann's music now lacks, and most of his stage work retains only the faded picturesqueness of the stock romantic figures and situations—the vikings, the trolls, the wood and water nymphs, the firelit caverns and the moonlit groves. It was the fate of both Hartmann and Gade to settle into a comfortable provincial round all too early in their long lives, and to go on writing prolifically with little development of technical resource while the larger musical world of Brahms and Wagner, Mussorgsky and Verdi passed them by. Their work is full of fine gestures and poetical ideas, but their range of expression is too circumscribed to prolong these golden moments.

Nevertheless, they founded a minor school of stage music whose best-known exponent was Edvard Grieg. His unfinished opera, *Olav Trygvason*, begun in 1873 to a text spasmodically produced by Bjørnson, is almost pure Hartmann, and the same ancestral features are discernible in Grieg's music to Bjørnson's

[1] Gosse, E., *Northern Studies*, 2nd edtn., London, 1883, pp. 154–5.

Bergliot (1871), to *Sigurd Jorsalfar* (1872)—also by Bjørnson—and to Ibsen's *Peer Gynt* (1874–5). The tradition is carried on in the incidental music of Svendsen and Halvorsen.

In the meantime, both Copenhagen and Stockholm had established themselves as centres of international opera. The Danish capital was fortunate in a succession of directors of the calibre of Schall, Glaeser, and Svendsen; while the Stockholm opera house could offer Jenny Lind, in her first seasons as *prima donna* from 1838 to 1841, roles in *Der Freischütz, Don Giovanni, Die Zauberflöte, Robert de Normandie, Lucia di Lammermoor,* and *Norma.* The arrival of Wagnerian music-drama on the northern stages not only revealed new worlds of dramatic and musical expression, but also gave a fresh impetus to the production of operatic works based on heroic national myths. Thus the Swedish composer Johan Andreas Hallén (1842–1925) shows very strongly the influence of Wagner in *Harald Viking* (produced in Leipzig in 1887) and still more in later works like *Häxfällan* and *Valdemarsskatten,* which represent an attempt to combine the style of *Tristan* with folk-music colouring. *Valdemarsskatten* ('The treasure of Waldemar'), written for the opening of the new opera house in Stockholm in April 1899, is a full-blooded late romantic drama in mediaeval Swedish setting, with attendant courtiers, monks, burghers and a walling-up scene to conclude the action for good measure. Perhaps the most ambitious Danish opera of this period was *Aladdin,* by Christian Frederik Emil Hornemann (1840–1906), whose style testifies to his admiration for Brahms, and who is considered to have had some influence on the stylistic development of Carl Nielsen.

Both in Norway and in Finland there were valiant attempts to create serious national opera. As far as Norway is concerned, the story is one of repeated frustration. Andreas Udbye (1820–1889), wrote a work entitled *Fredkulla,* which owing to a series of mishaps never reached performance. Ole Olsen (1850–1927) succeeded in getting a hearing for only one of his four operas; this was *Lajla,* which had a Lapland setting and was performed in Christiania in 1908, sharing the bill with the first stage production of Grieg's *Olav Trygvason.* Johannes Haarklou (1847–1925), an individualist of peasant stock but conventional Leipzig training, had two stage works produced—

Fra gamle Dage (1894) and *Marisaghet* (1910). A group of Norwegian composers including Christian Sinding, Sigwardt Asperstrand (1856–1942), and Gerhard Schjelderup (1859–1933) met with far more success in German opera houses than in their native country. The one operatic composer who has had better fortune is Arne Eggen (b. 1881); his *Olav Liljekrans*, first produced at the Oslo national theatre in 1940, has claims to be considered the first true Norwegian opera.

Finnish national opera begins in a sense as far back as 1852, when Fredrik Pacius produced *Kung Karls Jakt* to a Swedish text by Topelius; but it was not until the end of the century that the first opera to a libretto in the Finnish language was composed by Oskar Merikanto under the title of *Pohjan Nehti* ('The Maid of the North'). Since then the most successful Finnish operas have been those of Leevi Madetoja (1887–1947).

We may conclude this chapter with some notice of lighter forms of stage and *salon* entertainment that have become a part of Swedish and Danish musical traditions. The ponderous Wagnerian works of Hallén are relieved by the far less pretentious scores of Johan August Söderman (1832–1876), whose rustic idyll *Ett bondbröllop* ('A country wedding') has been described by Moses Pergament as the most Swedish of all Swedish music. Ivar Hallström (1826–1901) introduced a savour of Gallic wit into his long series of light operas, beginning with *Den Bergtagna* (1874). Lastly, we must refer to a Danish institution that has become known all over the world as a centre of the best light music in many forms. When in 1843 the ex-army officer and journalist Georg Carstensen opened the Tivoli pleasure-grounds in the heart of Copenhagen he had the foresight to engage a young band leader named H. C. Lumbye to provide entertainment in one of the pavilions. Lumbye had already been inspired by the success of Johann Strauss to form his own orchestra of twenty players and to compose waltzes, polkas and galops on the Viennese model. He also followed Strauss in exploiting exotic and realistic sound-effects. Altogether Lumbye wrote more than six hundred pieces of dance music, many with intriguing titles like 'Champagne Galop', 'Telegraph Galop', and 'Railway Galop', and he furnished some of Bournonville's ballets with music. Lumbye is still, after a hundred years, the tutelary genius of the Tivoli gardens, and his tunes are seldom absent from the lighter programmes given there.

10

Jean Sibelius and Carl
Nielsen

With the appearance of two composers of the calibre
of Sibelius and Carl Nielsen, both of whom were
born in 1865, the Scandinavian lands can be said
to approach the status, musically speaking, of Great Powers.
No longer is it a question of admitting the worth of lyric
miniatures, but of reckoning with symphonic structures impressive in dimensions and rugged of aspect, presenting a
defiant challenge to the musical experience of audiences and
critics whose own native traditions may be far more continuous
than those of Finland or Denmark. The challenge has not gone
unanswered, and controversy over the relative and absolute
merits of the two protagonists still flourishes, especially in the
English-speaking countries where interest in both, but particularly in Sibelius, has always been stronger than anywhere
outside Scandinavia itself.[1] In Britain there has been a falling-
off in the enthusiasm that accompanied Beecham's sponsorship
of the works of Sibelius in the nineteen-thirties, followed by a
reaction, during the middle years of the century, in favour of
Nielsen; recent changes of fashion, and a renewed admiration
for the late nineteenth-century Viennese symphonists, have
given rise to further questionings which clearly will not be
finally resolved until both the northerners can be seen further
off in the perspective of history.

[1] Recent studies include: Simpson, R., *Carl Nielsen, Symphonist*, London,
1952; Abraham, G. (edr.), *Sibelius: a Symposium*, London, 1947; Parmet, S.,
Sibelius' Symphonies, London, 1959; Johnson, H. E., *Sibelius*, London, 1960.

It would be hard to find greater diversity in social and educational backgrounds than the biographies of these two composers reveal. Jean Sibelius (1865–1957) came from a professional family, learnt Swedish as his mother tongue and Finnish as a second language, and had a conventional musical training, first under Wegelius at the Helsingfors Conservatory, and afterwards in Berlin and Vienna. In 1892, the year of his marriage, he came before the public as a national romantic composer, with the imposing orchestral and choral work *Kullervo*[1] and the tone-poem *En Saga*, and in the following year he produced the far more individual and intense orchestral piece *The Swan of Tuonela*, with its echoes of Wagner in the cor anglais melisma and of Grieg in the string writing, but also with its atmosphere of the brooding mythology of *Kalevala*. The second phase of Sibelius' personal and artistic development begins in 1897, with the award of a government stipend that set him free to devote the whole of his energies to composition; from this time, until the famous 'silence from Järvenpää' after his sixtieth year, the series of seven symphonies stretches like a mountain chain,[2] to be rounded off with the last and greatest of the *Kalevala* tone-poems, the awe-inspiring monothematic *Tapiola*. Political events—the First World War, during which the fifth symphony was written in its earlier form, the Finnish Civil War of 1919, the Second World War, and the subsequent war with Russia find no apparent reflection in the life and art of this enigmatical personality, nor are there traces of the cataclysmic revolutions in musical style associated with Schoenberg, Bartók and Stravinsky. The last thirty years of his life were almost totally unproductive, and the much talked of eighth symphony never materialized.

Carl Nielsen grew up in a peasant community on the Danish island of Funen, near Odense, the birthplace of Hans Andersen. The joys and privations of his early life, and his first musical

---

[1] This title had already been given to an overture by Filip von Schantz (1835–65), written in 1860 for the opening of a new theatre, and said to be the first full-scale orchestral work based on *Kalevala*. Other interesting precursors of Sibelius were Axel Gabriel Ingelius (1822–68), who wrote a symphony containing a 5/4 movement; and Ernst Mielck (1877–99).

[2] Symphony no. 1, 1899; no. 2, 1901; no. 3, 1907; no. 4, 1911; no. 5, 1915; no. 6, 1923; no. 7, 1924.

experiences, are most movingly described in the autobiographical sketch *My childhood in Funen (Min fynske Barndom)*. Service as a military band-boy (recalled, perhaps, in the side-drum episodes of the fourth and fifth symphonies) led on to a course at the Copenhagen Conservatory where Gade still reigned. Nielsen's first symphony, introduced to the public by Svendsen in 1894, preceded that of Sibelius by five years; thereafter the two composers kept almost exactly in step in their symphonic production. Carl Nielsen's second (*The Four Temperaments*) appeared in 1902; his third (*Sinfonia espansiva*) in 1912; his fourth (*Det Uuslukkelig* or *The Unquenchable*—for 'Inextinguishable' carries comic implications in English) in 1916; his fifth between 1920 and 1922; and his sixth and last (*Sinfonia semplice*) in 1925. It is seldom remembered that Carl Nielsen himself conducted the fourth symphony in London in 1923, and it was not until the Danish State Radio Orchestra gave a magnificent performance of the fifth at the Edinburgh Festival in 1950 that the British public woke to a realization of the possibility that Scandinavia might have given the world more than one major symphonist.

Though comparable in stature and reputation—and, it must be repeated, in the vicissitudes and local limitations of their fame—the two composers show profound differences of musical temperament arising partly from the natural and cultural environments in which they grew to maturity. Sibelius belonged to the Finnish race with its twin cultures, the Swedish and the Ugrian-Finnish, with yet a third in the background, that of European Russia, whose own origins were partly in the Scandinavian lands. As the years went on Sibelius seems to have encouraged the popular view of his personality as enigmatic, lonely, and introverted, drawing inspiration from nature, both directly and through the poetic medium of *Kalevala* with its mythology and nature symbolism. His tone-poems, and perhaps his symphonies also, belong to that superhuman, or subhuman, universe rather than to the life-size world of ordinary humanity.

Carl Nielsen, on the other hand, identifies himself with human comedy and tragedy, and is characteristically Danish in his frank enjoyment of the kindlier and warmer aspects of nature and humanity, in his mercurial temperament, and in the prolixity of his fancy. But it may prove fallacious to carry too far an examination of his music from a psychological standpoint. His main interest seems, after all, to be in the qualities of vocal and instrumental sound and in exploring fresh possibilities of combining them: 'The glutted must be taught to regard a melodic third as a gift of God, a fourth as an experience, and a fifth as the supreme bliss'; this observation of Carl Nielsen recalls the well-known remark by Sibelius about the glass of cold water. Both aphorisms are symptomatic of a revulsion against the later developments of German romanticism.

The musical structures of Sibelius have often been analysed and described. They involve great economy of material, with the creation of apparently undistinguished ideas which gradually reveal powers of inner development and outer coherence under the stress of an intense rhythmic drive and sense of climax. The time-span is made to appear all the greater through the tension of organic growth upon a foundation of slow but inevitable harmonic movement. Subordinate devices strengthen the feeling of progression over a vast time-scale: the long-drawn monotone that focuses attention on the moment and the means of its own release, the splendidly graduated crescendos. Carl Nielsen often displays no less ability to pile up tensions and climax; but he is more generous, even prodigal with his ideas, not all of which he necessarily carries into the later stages of development. Much has been made of his treatment of key systems; they are as firmly grounded in tonal harmony as those of Sibelius, but there are frequent and unpredictable deviations and often a gradual change of key-centre in the course of a lengthy movement without an eventual return to the starting-point. Whereas with Sibelius every note contributes towards a unified drive on an ultimate goal, in Carl Nielsen's major works there are diversions and interruptions, humorous or petulant according to the prevailing aspect of his musical temperament. The same quality of naïve excitement can be felt in Carl Nielsen's handling of instruments; sheer exultation in the technique of the woodwind, for example, gives many passages in his scores an improvisatorial character, and there is the famous point in the fifth symphony at which the side-drum player is directed to improvise an interruption to the movement's organic progression.

XXI Group of Scandinavian composers at the Festival of Nordic Music, Copenhagen, 1919. From left to right: Fredrik Schnedler-Petersen, Robert Kajanus, Jean Sibelius, George Hoeberg, Erkki Melartin, Wilhelm Stenhammar, Carl Nielsen, and Johan Halvorsen

XXII Hilding Rosenberg

Both composers are as individual in their scoring as in their structural methods. The orchestration of Sibelius, which he himself compared to granite, is characterized by a wonderfully rich treatment of the strings, which are often subdivided and weighted in the lower registers. The strings also are the usual means of producing the long and inexorable climaxes of the symphonies and tone-poems. Carl Nielsen, as a practical band and orchestral player—he was for a time a violinist in Det. Kgl. Kapel, and was one of Svendsen's successors at the conductor's desk of the Royal Theatre—habitually achieves the translucency that not only belongs to his whole cast of musical thought but also suggests affinities with older Scandinavian composers, such as Berwald and Svendsen. The general brilliance of orchestral effect is enhanced by the mobility of Carl Nielsen's harmonic language, in contrast to the generally slower harmonic rhythm of Sibelius and his use of prolonged pedal basses.

While the symphonies dominate the work of both composers, there are other fields that claim attention. Sibelius left only one chamber work of importance, the string quartet *Voces intimae* (1909), but Carl Nielsen published no fewer than four string quartets, of which the third, written in 1896, was dedicated to Grieg; two violin and piano sonatas; and a late wind quintet (1922) which ends with a set of variations on the composer's own setting of a hymn by Grundtvig. A quotation from the second sonata for violin and piano (1912), admittedly one of Nielsen's more 'difficult' works, illustrates the individual character of his tonal language and the subtlety of his rhythmic organization:

Reproduced by permission of Wilhelm Hansen, Copenhagen.

The language bar has prevented much of the vocal music of either composer from becoming familiar outside their own countries, and the rest of the world has thereby been cut off from some of their finest work. Sibelius showed his quality as a song-writer even in his earliest published composition, a setting of a *Serenad* by Runeberg with an unexpected resemblance to the style of Fauré. In his later songs, and particularly those to Finnish words, there is less grace and more austerity, with a mode of declamation that derives from the *runo* singing of Finnish folk music. Carl Nielsen's songs are fewer than those of Sibelius, and even less known because seldom translated. They are strongly Danish in atmosphere and often, as in the Ludvig Holstein songs (op. 10), of touching beauty. Neither Sibelius nor Carl Nielsen is in the habit of using direct folk song quotation, but not only is their work, both vocal and instrumental, moulded by the rhythms and cadences of folk song, but they have also enriched their peoples with compositions in folk song style, particularly for that favourite Scandinavian institution, the male voice students' choir. Carl Nielsen has produced more extended choral works in *Hymnus Amoris* (1896), inspired by a study of Palestrina, whose influence was also acknowledged by Sibelius; and the charming *Fynske Foraar* ('Springtime in Funen') (1921) inspired by the warm fruitfulness of the Danish composer's native island.

The bond of brotherhood between musician and dramatist that is so strong in Scandinavian cultural history is again apparent in the long series of scores prepared by Sibelius for theatrical productions and culminating in the music for Shakespeare's *Tempest*, written for the Royal Theatre, Copenhagen, and first performed in 1926. Carl Nielsen also wrote music for plays, including Oehlenschläger's *Aladdin* (1918); and he created a classic of Danish comic opera in *Maskarade* (1906), founded on one of Holberg's plays, and attempted a weightier biblical opera, with important choral sections, in *Saul og David*, first produced in 1902.

While neither composer has shown himself to be aware of the subtler aspects of pianoforte music, nor to have written idiomatically for that instrument, both turned frequently to the keyboard: Sibelius mainly for slight pieces of the *salon* kind, but Carl Nielsen for large-scale compositions that attempt to carry on the contrapuntal and variation techniques of Beethoven and Brahms. In all Nielsen wrote four big works for the piano: the *Symphonic Suite* (op. 8), which is the one most strongly indebted to Brahms; the *Chaconne* (op. 32); the *Tema med Variationer* (op. 40); and the *Suite* (op. 45), all of which are not only considerable accessions to the literature of the instrument but also have given rise to a series of works in the same *genre* both in Denmark, where they have their successors in the larger piano works of Niels Viggo Bentzon, and in Sweden, where Hilding Rosenberg has treated the piano on a similarly broad scale and with similar disregard of the more sensuous and impressionistic qualities of pianoforte sound. In complete and characteristic contrast are Carl Nielsen's interesting five-finger piano pieces (*Klavermusik for Smaa og Store*) which appeared in 1930, a year before the monumental organ piece *Commotio*, his last published work and one we have already referred to as linking modern Danish music with the baroque linear style of Buxtehude.

I I

Norwegian Music after Grieg

A change from romanticism to realism in literature and
the arts was general throughout Scandinavia during the
last three or four decades of the nineteenth century, but
was hastened or retarded by factors that differed from country
to country. In Sweden a major dramatist, August Strindberg
(1849–1912), reached the summit of his powers in a series of
naturalistic plays written during the eighties. In Denmark the
process was accelerated by the war with Germany and the loss
of Slesvig in 1864, and by the writings of Georg Brandes (1842–
1927) with his demand for a *Gennembrud* or 'break-through' of
the romantic barrier. In Norway the literary apostles of realism
and naturalism began as national romantics; Camilla Collet
(1813–1895) was the sister of the nationalist poet Wergeland,
and it was not until the eighteen-sixties that Henrik Ibsen and
Bjørnstjerne Bjørnson turned away from stories and plays in
picturesque rural and historical settings to current social,
moral and psychological problems. As far as music was concerned, Norway never experienced the headlong flight from
national romanticism that was to occur in Denmark and
Sweden.

One reason for this is that however strongly Grieg's successors
may have wished to avoid the more subjective and sentimental
elements in his style, it was Grieg himself who provided, in his
last compositions, the materials for a reaction: namely, the
vitality of genuine folk music in the *slåtter*, in contrast to the
drawing-room or concert-hall refinement of folk-idioms in his
earlier piano pieces, and an enlarged harmonic and rhythmic
vocabulary that links a specialized regional tradition with the

wider and more complex worlds of Stravinsky, Bartók, and Schoenberg.

Secondly, the German occupation of Norway during 1940–44 produced an intensified nationalism which had its defensive and its aggressive sides; the magnificent scenery of Norway, for example, was no longer merely a picturesque setting for remote history and legend but had become a formidable modern weapon against the invader, and at the same time a symbol of spiritual independence. Folk music, far from being a precious or a dying cult, increased in popularity, and survivals like the *hardingfele* and the traditional tunes and styles associated with it gained fresh ground. A further consequence of the invasion was that art became closely interwoven with politics, and a musician's personal attitudes during the years of trial coloured his compatriots' assessment of the intrinsic value of his work.

Traditional music, especially that of the *hardingfele*, formed part of the early environment of Harald Saeverud (b. 1897), some of whose ancestors were makers and players of that instrument. His first symphony was performed in Oslo in 1920, and in 1933 a state pension enabled him to give all his time to composition. Besides writing a number of symphonies and concertos, Saeverud has been inspired by folk music to create works for orchestra and for piano based on *slåtter* idioms: the piano pieces entitled *Slåtter og Stev fra Siljustøl* and an orchestral piece in the form of a passacaglia and entitled *Galdreslatten* (1947), are examples. In 1948 Saeverud wrote new incidental music for *Peer Gynt* with the aim of 'deromanticizing' the associations that Grieg's familiar score had woven around Ibsen's satirical and psychological drama. In the second piano concerto (1948–50) many of the harmonic, rhythmic and melodic ideas spring from the *slåtter*, and the procedure of working up a movement from a quiet start gradually to the full. power of soloist and orchestra is suggestive of the peasant musician's processional dance or *gangar*. Yet another feature, and one that Saeverud shares with several of his Norwegian contemporaries, is the persistent use of dotted rhythms, a marked feature of *slåtter*; the following example is taken from one of Saeverud's piano sonatinas for children:

Allegretto scherzando

Reproduced by permission of Musikk-huset A/S, Oslo.

These folk music traits may be more clearly apparent, however, to a detached observer than to the composer himself, who has always denied the direct influence of folk-idioms on his work, though he is conscious of having absorbed the spirit of the Norwegian tradition.

Spiritually also he gained much from the Norwegian Resistance movement, and his Ballad of Revolt (*Kjæmpeviseslåtten*) for orchestra (originally piano) has become popular not only in Norway but also in other lands, such as Israel, where strong feelings of national independence seek expression. An even more important product of the Resistance period is the symphonic trilogy, made up of the composer's fifth, sixth and seventh symphonies, all written in the war years and having references to the struggle in their subtitles.

Slåtter intervals, scales and rhythms are prominent in the music of Klaus Egge (b. 1906), whose first mature compositions were heard in Oslo about five years before the war. He completed a symphony during the occupation, and at the same time became president of the Norwegian Composers' Society. He has written two piano concertos, a violin concerto, three symphonies, a symphonic poem *Sveinung Vreim*, string and wind quartets, and a piano sonata, *Draumkvedesonate*, a powerfully imaginative reinterpretation of the mediaeval Norwegian ballad of heaven and hell, based on traditional tunes but written in a dissonant linear idiom with typical *hardingfele* figuration; the quotation below is from the beginning of the last movement, with a folk-ballad tune in the middle of the texture:

Reproduced by permission of Musikkhuset A/S, Oslo.

The inspiration of mediaeval ballads and religious poetry is apparent also in the work of Sparre Olsen (b. 1903), who like Klaus Egge was a pupil of the most original of all twentieth-century Norwegian composers, Fartein Valen. Olsen's orchestral works include a symphony and variations on a folk-tune, and there are two interesting choral cantatas, one of them a setting of *Draumkvedet* and the other of a mystical Latin poem, *Ver sanctum*.

Ludvig Irgens Jensen (b. 1894) is known chiefly as a composer in large-scale forms derived from the baroque and classical periods. Examples are the orchestral *Passacaglia* (1926–8), which culminates in a triple fugue; the 'dramatic symphony' *Heimferd* ('Home-coming') written for the St. Olav commemoration at Trondheim in 1930; and the symphony in D minor, written in 1942 and again ending with a triple fugue. Perhaps the most widely known of all Jensen's works is the *Partita sinfonica* (1939).

Bjarne Brustad (b. 1895) has attempted to handle folk material in the manner of Bartók and Hindemith, using ostinato figures of accompaniment and a harmonic language that includes experiments in bitonality. A large part of his production is built round the violin and viola, on which instruments he is a concert performer. There are two violin concertos, an *Eventyrsvit* (folk-tale suite) for solo violin, a Norse sonata for violin and piano, a *Capriccio* for violin and viola, a concertino for viola and orchestra, and a suite for solo viola. Brustad has also composed three symphonies and a series of choral works with orchestra.

Eivind Groven (b. 1901) is a native of Telemark, one of the strongholds of traditional music, and is a modern exponent of the *hardingfele*. His major works include a symphony (1946) and a piano concerto (1950). He has done much to preserve and disseminate Norwegian folk music, and is particularly interested in the acoustics of natural scales, which he demonstrates by means of an organ giving automatically-controlled non-tempered intervals.

Geirr Tveitt (b. 1908) has likewise combined an ardent interest in folk music and its scalar systems with prolific composition in the larger forms, including the piano concerto, of which he has produced five examples. He has collected and arranged an immense number of tunes from the Hardanger region, and has composed a concerto for Hardanger fiddle and orchestra. Not least among his many talents is a brilliant flair for instrumental colour.

Standing apart from all his contemporaries in Scandinavia was Fartein Valen (1887–1953), one of the most interesting figures in twentieth-century music.[1] His father was one of those 'missionaries from Stavanger' shunned by the Devil in the last act of *Peer Gynt*, and young Valen spent some impressionable years of childhood among the luxuriant flora and fauna of Madagascar. His serious musical studies began in Oslo under Catherinus Elling, and at the same time he read modern languages and philosophy at the university. Later he went to Berlin, took lessons from Max Bruch, heard Reger play his own piano works, and was enthralled by a performance of Schoenberg's early quartet in D minor (op. 7). Both Reger and Schoenberg seem to have contributed to the development of Valen's intricate linear style of polyphony which he applied alike to vocal, keyboard, and orchestral composition. His melodic structure and use of dissonance soon became as bold as Schoenberg's, although he never adopted a systematic serial technique.

Valen's sonata for violin and piano (op. 3, composed 1916)

[1] For a full biographical and critical study, see Gurvin, Olav, *Fartein Valen: en banebryter i nyere norsk musikk. Oslo*, 1962.

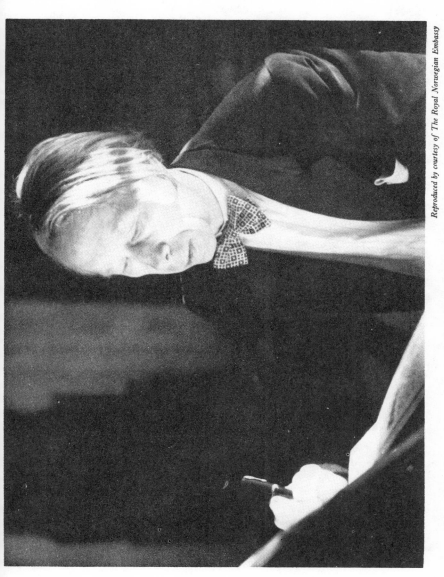

XXIII Harald Saeverud

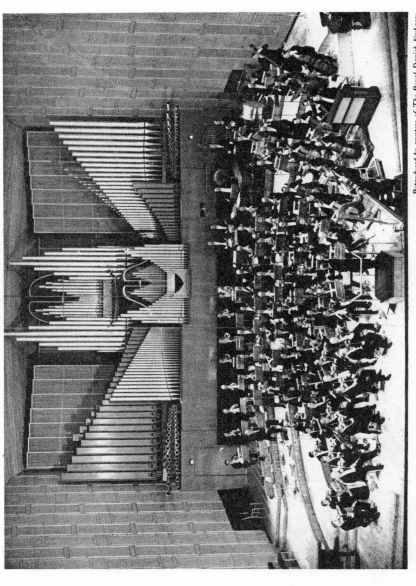

XXIV The Royal Danish State Radio Symphony Orchestra in the Concert Hall, Radio House, Copenhagen

and his piano trio (op. 5, written between 1917 and 1924) are works of strong individuality, marking a process of transition from a partially tonal language to a completely emancipated twelve-note idiom that may be conveniently illustrated from the theme (in mirror form) and opening variation of the piano variations (op. 23, finished 1936):

Reproduced by permission of Harald Lyche & Co.s Musikkforlag, Oslo.

It is characteristic of Valen's intensive methods of work that he devoted almost a whole year to the composition of these variations. Throughout his life he subjected himself to the severest technical discipline, as when, for example, he compelled himself to play all the Bach '48' in every key and then to write six fugues of his own on *each* of the Bach fugue subjects.[1]

Through shorter orchestral pieces like *Le Cimitière marin*, inspired by a Spanish translation of Valéry's poem and by the discovery of a neglected graveyard near Valen's own home, and *La Isla de las Calmas*, an impression of a beautiful scene off the island of Majorca, Valen began to attempt works on a larger scale. After settling on his estate at Valestrand in western Norway in 1938, he produced four symphonies (and part of a fifth),

[1] Gurvin, *op. cit.*, p. 58.

a violin concerto of remarkably close-knit construction, a wind serenade, and a piano concerto (completed in 1951), the year before his death. His lifelong devotion to religious mysticism was expressed in a setting for soprano and orchestra of a German version of *La Noche oscura del Alma*, by St. John of the Cross.[1]

Despite his asceticism, both personal and artistic, Valen has always been respected and admired by his fellow-musicians in Norway, and latterly his sensitive and subtle idiom and technical integrity have caused much of his work to be performed and studied in other countries.

---

[1] Written in 1939 and dedicated to the Norwegian composer and critic Pauline Hall on her fiftieth birthday.

12

Danish Music after Carl Nielsen

Following the earliest disciples of Carl Nielsen, who included Rudolf Simonsen, Peder Gram, Poul Schierbeck and Emilius Bangert—all born in the eighteen-eighties— came a generation less directly indebted but none the less united in their regard for his personality and artistic aims and methods. With this younger generation may be included the eminent musicologist Knud Jeppesen (b. 1890) who is known internationally for his doctoral thesis *The Style of Palestrina and the Dissonance*[1] and his textbook on *Counterpoint*, but who is also a composer of important works, including a symphony, a horn concerto, a work for organ, *Intonazione boreale*, inspired by Carl Nielsen's *Commotio*, and an impressive *Te Deum Danicum* written in 1945 for the inauguration of the concert hall of the State Radio.

A pupil of Jeppesen and Thomas Laub in Denmark, and of Joseph Marx in Vienna, Finn Høffding (b. 1899) has given valuable service to educational causes and has written stage and choral music for amateurs on lines suggested by the work of Hindemith and Fritz Jöde. His early symphonies, four in number, show him as a follower of Carl Nielsen; his later output contains interesting experiments in chamber music like the *Dialogues* for oboe and clarinet. One of the most popular of his orchestral pieces is entitled *Det er ganske vist . . .* ('It is quite true . . .') after the beginning of one of Hans Andersen's tales.

Jørgen Bentzon (1897–1951) studied with Carl Nielsen and Karg-Elert, and also undertook a legal training that eventually

[1] Published in German in 1922, in an English version in 1927.

143

secured him a post in the Ministry of Justice. Although he wrote several big works including two symphonies and an opera, *Saturnalia* (1944), he showed a preference for small ensembles giving clear-cut melodic lines, as in the sonata for flute, clarinet and bassoon, the *Variazioni interrotti* for clarinet, bassoon and three stringed instruments, and the series of *Racconti*, each in one movement, for groups of three to five instruments, the texture being polyphonic and each part preserving the special character of the instrument concerned.

The present Director of the Royal Danish Conservatory, Knudaage Riisager, is cosmopolitan in background; born in 1897 of Danish parents then living in Russia, he studied first in Denmark and later in Germany, where he acquired a taste for the baroque period. He also went to Paris, took lessons with Roussel and met Ravel. His own writing shows a Gallic brilliance and wit, and his sympathies with French ideals have had a stimulating effect on modern Danish music. The lengthy list of his compositions includes four symphonies, but it is by his lighter works that he is chiefly known. The concertino for trumpet and strings and the string partita are examples, already popular outside Denmark, of Riisager's entertaining style, which often recalls that of Poulenc. His most important contribution to the ballet is a triptych, comprising *Tolv med Posten* ('twelve by the post'), another Hans Andersen tale; *Slaraffenland*, based on the Breughel picture of the Paradise of Fools; and *Qartsiluni*, an impressionist piece suggested by Greenland Eskimo folklore.

Two other Danish musicians who owe much to French influences are Svend Erik Tarp (b. 1908), composer of a serenade for flute, clarinet, violin, and 'cello, a concerto for flute, a *Te Deum*, and a symphony (1949), and editor of a society for the publication of Danish music; and Jørgen Jersild (b. 1913), another pupil of Roussel and a gifted composer and teacher who has published some useful textbooks.

A salient characteristic of the twentieth-century Danish school—a prolific output of works in the larger forms—can be observed in the careers of three composers who are all in their several ways linked with the Carl Nielsen tradition. The oldest of the group, Herman D. Koppel (b. 1904), has written five symphonies, three concertos for piano, one for 'cello, and one for clarinet, and three string quartets and other chamber works, besides the radio and film scores that most modern Scandinavian musicians are called upon to produce. His sympathies with the Jewish race and his distress at their sufferings in the world war inspired his third symphony and his settings of some of the psalms. Svend S. Schultz (b. 1913), though best known outside Denmark for a serenade for strings, also has a long list of ambitious works to his credit, including several symphonies and a series of chamber operas. Niels Viggo Bentzon (b. 1919) has given particular attention to the piano, which he plays as a concert artist and for which he has written a number of pieces in extended forms, which can be regarded as direct successors of Carl Nielsen's big keyboard works. But Bentzon has also composed a great deal for the orchestra—his symphonies some time ago reached the classic number of nine—and for smaller combinations of instruments treated in neo-baroque style, as in the chamber concerto for three pianos, clarinet, bassoon, two trumpets, contrabass and percussion.

One of the outstanding figures of twentieth-century Danish music is Vagn Holmboe, who was born in Jutland in 1909. His earlier studies in Copenhagen under Knud Jeppesen and Finn Høffding helped to give him an insight into the continuing vitality of seventeenth- and eighteenth-century principles of composition, together with a deep admiration for the symphonies and quartets of Carl Nielsen. An entirely different set of influences was added when Holmboe travelled in Germany, to continue his studies under Ernst Toch, and in Rumania, where he became absorbed in the musical personality of Bartók and in Bartók's researches into the folk music of Eastern Europe.

These diverse experiences rapidly became fused together by Holmboe's powerful creative gifts. His skill in Palestrinian counterpoint was exercised in choral and instrumental polyphony, his interest in eighteenth-century textures led to the production of twelve chamber concerti for solo instruments, or groups of soloists, with small orchestra, and his assimilation of many of the elements of Bartók's dissonant harmony and folk-inspired rhythms was combined with an attitude towards symphonic writing inherited from Carl Nielsen. Holmboe's human sympathies, like those of Nielsen, are warm and his sense of dedication is strong; composition is no esoteric language, but a means of communication, and much of his mature work grew out of the sufferings of oppressed people in the Second World War.

The nine symphonies form the core of Holmboe's work. The second, completed in 1939, gained an award from Det kgl. Kapelle. The third, *Sinfonia rustica*, recalls the enjoyment of orchestral sound and uninhibited tonal melody so characteristic of Carl Nielsen. The fourth, *Sinfonia sacra*, begun during the early years of the war, expresses 'the yearnings and invocations of the suppressed peoples of the world in 1941'. The fifth symphony, likewise written under stress of war, is charged with emotion and is technically closely knit through the use of thematic metamorphosis. In the sixth symphony, organization becomes even more thorough and the entire work is cast in a single continuous movement; and in the seventh and eighth symphonies there is further exploration of the techniques of metamorphosis and variation.

Holmboe's chamber music is of equal interest. It includes works for wind quintet and a series of string quartets whose background is shared by Carl Nielsen and Béla Bartók. Apart from a comparatively early quartet (not now recognized by the composer as part of the canon) the series begins with three quartets all written in 1949 after a performance of Bartók's sixth quartet heard in Copenhagen; the first is dedicated to Bartók *in memoriam*, the second speaks with a convincing Hungarian accent, but in the third Holmboe's own personality fully asserts itself, with a wide range of feeling through the five movements and a remarkable use of the chaconne in the central movement, where serial procedure is reconciled with a language that retains its tonal basis.

It is unfortunate that, owing to a number of circumstances, Vagn Holmboe's music is so difficult to become well acquainted with at the present time in Britain. None of it is available in current recordings, and scores are seldom obtainable without special order from Denmark. Here is a composer who would repay closer attention, for, in the words of a Danish critic, 'His mastery of musical rhetoric is intense, borne as it is by a pathos, a passion, and a formal control rarely found in these days, and as elemental as they are spirited.'[1]

[1] Kappel, V., *Danish Music from the Lur to the Vibraphone* (second series), Copenhagen, 1951.

One of the youngest Danish composers to obtain recognition outside Scandinavia is Bernhard Lewkovitch (b. 1927), who holds the appointment of organist and choirmaster at St. Ansgar's Roman Catholic cathedral in Copenhagen. His reputation rests chiefly on his choral music, which includes three psalms to Latin words, two masses—one (op. 10) *a capella* and the other (op. 15) with wind and harp, three motets to Danish words, and five Italian madrigals. In these short but impressive compositions there is a strong sense of national choral tradition, linking modern free tonality with the vocal writing of Knud Jeppesen and Carl Nielsen, and further back with the motets and madrigals of Mogens Pedersøn:

('Lord, thou turnest my sorrow to dancing.')

Reproduced by permission of Wilhelm Hansen, Copenhagen.

13

Finnish Music after Sibelius

The tremendous personality of Sibelius dominated the music of Finland so completely for nearly half a century that few of his contemporaries escaped his influence in the formation of their style, in their choice of media and handling of form, and in their indebtedness to national literature. Only in the field of opera, which Sibelius hardly touched, were they able to supplement their master's achievement. We have already referred to the pioneer work of Oskar Merikanto (1868–1934) in creating the first Finnish opera. To the same generation belong Erkki Melartin (1875–1937), composer of *Aino*, an opera on a story from *Kalevala*, besides symphonies and chamber music; and Leevi Madetoja (1887–1947), who holds a position in the esteem of his countrymen which is perhaps second only to that of Sibelius himself. Madetoja's regional background (he was born near the Gulf of Bothnia) is strong in such works as the operas, *Pohjalaisia* ('The Bothnians') (1924) and *Juha* (1935), and in the tone-poem *Kullervo* (1913), and also in his many cantatas, choral pieces and solo songs. The opening of his song, *Jää hyvästi* ('Farewell'), shows an instance of the detached phrasing of the *runo* style which occurs likewise in the Finnish songs of Sibelius and Kilpinen. (See page 149.)

Madetoja also produced a large amount of orchestral music, including three symphonies, described as 'the most successful efforts at coping with the form in Finnish symphonic literature after Sibelius'.[1]

---

[1] Helasvuo, Veikko, *Sibelius and the Music of Finland*, 2nd edtn., Helsinki, 1957.

('My darling, farewell; tears fill my eyes.') (Words by L. Onerva.)

Reproduced by permission of Oy R. E. Westerlund AB, Helsinki.

149

Two minor composers who achieved international reputations, and whose names are therefore better known outside Finland than any others except Sibelius, are Armas Järnefelt (1869–1958) and Selim Palmgren (1878–1951). Järnefelt, who became a Swedish subject in 1910, was an operatic conductor whose fame as a composer rests almost entirely on two charming light orchestral pieces, *Praeludium* and *Berceuse*. Palmgren's choral music and songs are cherished in Finland, but abroad his name is associated chiefly with some well-turned piano pieces in the late romantic tradition; these had a long run of popularity both in England and in America, where Palmgren held a post at the Eastman School of Music.

Finnish music sustained a severe loss when Toivo Kuula (1883–1918) perished during the war of independence. Although Kuula did not live to develop a true twentieth-century style, but wrote in an idiom derived from Brahms, Dvořák, and Sibelius, with some influence from the French impressionists, his chamber music had great vitality and passionate spontaneity, as in the following melody from the piano trio (op. 7, 1908):

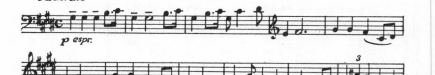

Reproduced by permission of Wilhelm Hansen, Copenhagen.

Finland shares with her Scandinavian neighbours a continuous and rich outpouring of lyrical song from the early years of the nineteenth century; Sibelius might have been remembered for his work in this field even if he had written nothing else, and few of his contemporaries and successors have failed to add to the store of settings of Finnish and Swedish lyric poetry. But Finland has one composer who has devoted himself almost entirely to song-writing: this is Yrjö Kilpinen (1892–1959), the number of whose published songs exceeds six hundred. Kilpinen was a traditionalist, with little interest in twentieth-century developments in tonal language or in vocal declamation. He drew, however, upon more than one tradition of solo song: at times he follows the German romantic *Lied*, at times the Scandinavian *romanse* with its more subdued emotional range and strophic pattern. In some of the Finnish songs he takes a folk-tune or *runo* as his starting-point and extends and elaborates it. Everywhere there is a confident understanding of what is vocally effective, combined with a plastic rhythmical sense and a fertility in ideas for keyboard figuration that gives every accompaniment its individual character.

The work of Aare Merikanto (1893–1958) marks a stage of transition from the ripe romanticism of the Finnish contemporaries of Sibelius, a group to which his father, Oskar Merikanto, belonged. Aare Merikanto's student days were spent in three countries—Finland, Germany, and Russia. In the period between the two world wars he gradually modified his earlier and rather conservative style and developed a post-romantic, but still recognizably personal idiom. His reputation as an orchestral composer stands high in Finland, and the list of his major works is imposing, with three symphonies, three violin concertos, two piano concertos, two 'cello concertos, a symphonic fantasy, and a tone-poem *Lemminkäinen*.

A similar process of adaptation was followed by Väinö Raitio (1891–1945), who contributed several operas to the Finnish stage. In his instrumental tone-pictures, his ballet music, and such larger works as the double concerto for violin and 'cello, his style and technique show his indebtedness to the French impressionist school; his use of the orchestra is brilliant, and his fantasy ranges widely, as indicated by titles such as *Fantasia estatica*, *Moonlight on Jupiter*, and *Felis domestica*.

Uuno Klami (1900–1961) began his career with comparatively little interest in the national-romantic enthusiasm shared by most of his compatriots at that time, his professional training having been almost entirely abroad, with Ravel in Paris and Willner in Vienna. It was Kajanus who persuaded him to attempt a work based on *Kalevala*; the result was a five-movement *Kalevala* suite for orchestra (1933, but revised considerably during the next ten years). An orchestral piece, with the almost inevitable title *Lemminkäinen*, originally designed as part of the suite, was given an independent existence in 1935. Klami also wrote three symphonies, two piano concertos, two works for 'cello with orchestra, and several overtures, all showing a brilliant flair for orchestral colour and effect.

Tauno Pylkkänen (b. 1918) studied at the Sibelius Academy and later in Italy and France, and the contrast between these Latin countries and the remote regions of northern Europe inspired his tone poem *Ultima Thule*, written in 1949. But his high reputation in Finland rests mainly on his operatic work; one of his operas, *Vargbruden* ('The wolf's bride'), was a prize-winner in an international competition organized by the Italian radio in 1950.

Ahti Sonninen (b. 1914) is an example of a Finnish composer remaining loyal to the nationalist tradition he inherited from his teachers, Palmgren and Aare Merikanto, and he has drawn extensively upon *Kalevala* mythology. In 1952 he wrote a ballet, *Pessi and Ilusia*, with a story based on Finnish folklore by the modern writer Yrjo Kokko. Sonninen has also produced concertos for piano and for violin, symphonic sketches for orchestra, and many choral and solo songs.

Some of the chamber music of Lauri Saikkola (b. 1905), including a *Divertimento* for wind quintet, and also his string suite (*Musica per archi*) with its Bartokian under-currents, have attracted attention outside Finland; his symphonies are less familiar, and the same observations apply to Nils-Eric Ringbom (b. 1907), who is better known through his *Miniature Suite* for orchestra and his wind sextet than through his symphonic works.

Erik Bergman (b. 1911), a Finnish exponent of twelve-tone composition, also has a wide reputation as a choral conductor, and has produced a setting of the *Rubaiyat* of Omar Khayyám for baritone, male voice choir, and orchestra. Great virtuosity is displayed in the symphonies and piano concerto of Einar Englund (b. 1916), and this quality finds even more scope in his theatre scores, with their fluent command of modern light music idioms. Eino Rautavaara (b. 1928) is a pupil of Aare Merikanto, and also studied with Aaron Copland in the United States, where he won an award for his *Requiem for our Time* for wind ensemble.

Finally, the work of three Finnish musicologists should be

mentioned. Ilmari Krohn (1867–1960), who became Professor at Helsinki University in 1918, made valuable studies of Finnish folk song and hymnology, besides· writing a series of textbooks in Finnish; Otto Andersson (b. 1879), Professor at the Åbo Academy, wrote a definitive monograph on *The Bowed Harp*;[1] and Toivo Haapanen (1889–1950), Krohn's successor in the chair at Helsinki, was an authority on mediaeval church music and on Finnish musical history in general. In the following words he expresses a truth that most of his countrymen will probably accept: 'It can be said that her music has most directly and to the greatest extent spread knowledge abroad about Finland's native culture.'[2]

[1] London, 1930.
[2] Quoted in Helasvuo, *Sibelius and the Music of Finland*, p. 95.

14

Wilhelm Stenhammar and Modern
Swedish Music

In 1919 Carl Nielsen was in Göteborg, conducting the Musical Association (Konstforeningen) concerts jointly with Wilhelm Stenhammar. This partnership is historically significant, as it brings together the names of two men who were to exert the strongest influence on contemporary Danish and Swedish music. Wilhelm Stenhammar (1871–1927) was descended on his mother's side from King Gustav Vasa, and there was always something aristocratic in his personal bearing and musical craftsmanship. His training as pianist and composer brought him into contact with Richard Andersson, Sjögren and Hallén in his native country, and with some of the greatest German musicians of the period. He admired Liszt, Wagner, Bruckner, and most of all Brahms, whose imprint stands clearly enough on Stenhammar's first piano concerto (B flat minor, 1894). An opera based on Ibsen's *Gildet paa Solhaug* dates from the same period, and like several other Scandinavian operas received its first performance in Germany. On returning to Sweden, Stenhammar soon built up a reputation as a concert pianist and chamber music player, outstanding in his interpretations of Beethoven, Schubert and Brahms.

There is still a great deal of Brahms in Stenhammar's second piano concerto (D minor, 1904–7), but his growing interest in the northern symphonists, Berwald, Carl Nielsen, and Sibelius, began to affect his earlier German sympathies and to modify his own style, producing a firmer texture and more controlled expression. His finest period as a composer dates from about

154

1910, and includes his fifth (1910) and sixth (1916) string quartets, and also the *Serenade* for orchestra (1918) and the G minor symphony. The sixth quartet shows Stenhammar moving towards a phase of still tauter writing, with a habit of harmonic ellipsis that has much in common with the style of Fauré in his last works:

Reproduced by permission of Wilhelm Hansen, Copenhagen.

Folk music in its natural state held little interest for Stenhammar, though the gentle melancholy of so much Swedish song, and the springing rhythms of so many Swedish dances, found their way into much of his work. He distrusted the idealization of peasant culture by members of an urbanized society. His aim was to bring Swedish music into the more powerful currents of contemporary European thought. He belongs to the age of realism in Sweden, the age of Strindberg, Heidenstam and Levertin; it was a psychological realism that strove for concentrated expression through verbal or pictorial symbols. Stenhammar's song-writing occupies an important position in his work, and arises from his responsiveness to modern Swedish poetry from Runeberg to Bo Bergman.

The origins of the modern Swedish school, therefore, can be traced to Stenhammar; nevertheless the spirit of national romanticism remained very much alive both in his generation and, as we shall see, during the one that followed. There was a time, not far distant, when such a figure as Wilhelm Peterson-Berger (1867–1942) had a strong following, though most discerning critics realized that his lyric talent and his fondness for picturesque programme material and folk-tune themes could not sustain the weight of his five symphonies and his series of nationalist music-dramas written in emulation of Wagner. His prolific output included nineteen books of Swedish songs. Another musician with strong literary interests was Anders Johan Ture Rangström (1884–1947), who was a close friend of Strindberg and Bo Bergman, and beside a large number of songs wrote a series of tone-poems with poetical titles and four symphonies, all based on literary or picturesque ideas: the first was a tribute to Strindberg. Rangström had little professional technique, but relied on some pictorial or verbal stimulus to set his creative processes in motion. Hugo Alfvén (b. 1872) on the other hand, worked successfully as a solo violinist and conductor, took Richard Strauss as his model, and learnt to write fluently for the large romantic orchestra. His five symphonies remained unknown abroad, but his folk-tune rhapsodies, and especially *Midsommarvaka*, have become part of the international repertory of light orchestral music. The final phase of Swedish romanticism, with its German affiliations, is represented by Natanael Berg (1879–1957), who became the first president of the Swedish Composers' Association and wrote a series of programme symphonies and several operas based on his own libretti.

Another group of Stenhammar's contemporaries shows the beginning of a neo-classical reaction. Kurt Atterberg (b. 1887) attracted much attention for the sixth of his nine symphonies, which won the Schubert centennial prize in 1928. He also produced four concertos (for violin, 'cello, horn and piano respectively), four operas, and a ballet, *De fåvitska Jungfrurna* ('The foolish virgins'). Adolf Wiklund (1879–1950) had much in common with Stenhammar, being like him an accomplished conductor and pianist, composer of two well-written piano concertos, and possessor of a restrained romantic style with recognizable Scandinavian colouring, as in the quasi-modal opening of the first piano concerto. Wiklund also wrote a symphony and other orchestral works, some chamber music, and a number of songs. Edvin Kallstenius (b. 1881) has had a long creative life, beginning with two string quartets in 1904–5 and continuing well into the second half of the century with such contemporary-sounding titles as *Sinfonietta dodicitona* (1956) and *Piccolo trio seriale* for flute, clarinet and cor anglais (1956).

For much valuable information about the development of contemporary music in Sweden one turns to the critical writings of Moses Pergament (b. 1893), who is himself a composer. Pergament has described[1] how the performance of Hilding Rosenberg's first string quartet in 1923 before a bewildered audience of Stockholm music critics marked the beginning of a new era; and he sketches the composer's biography and artistic career up to that point. Hilding Rosenberg was born at Ringsjön in Skåne in 1892. His father was head gardener at the castle of Bosjökloster, and had musical gifts that he passed on to several of his sons. The family sang in the local church choir and played various instruments. Hilding soon became proficient on the organ, piano and violin, and in his early twenties moved to Stockholm, where Richard Andersson introduced him to contemporary French and Spanish music.

It was after the composition of his first symphony in 1917 that Rosenberg met Wilhelm Stenhammar, who took a lively interest in his work and gave him lessons. Other encounters followed. A hearing of Sibelius' first symphony—a work that had been hissed at a performance in Göteborg in 1912—made a lasting impression on Rosenberg, a visit to Dresden in 1920 brought him into contact with Schoenberg, and a six months' sojourn in Paris culminated in the writing of his first string quartet; this was the first of Rosenberg's works to show the influence of Schoenberg, and Moses Pergament calls it the composer's unripe fruit, interesting mainly as evidence of his absorption in a new and stimulating idiom.

By taking up again the study of Bach's counterpoint in the light of Schoenberg's linear style, Rosenberg was able to free himself altogether from romanticist associations and gain full command of a firm modern technique. Among the works that followed this liberation were the sonata for violin alone; a trio for flute, violin and viola and one for oboe, clarinet and bassoon; the four piano sonatas; a suite and a sonata for violin and piano; the chamber symphony; and two more string

[1] In *Svenska Tonsättare*, Stockholm, 1943, pp. 102 seq.

quartets. All these displayed the expressionist attitude and linear texture accepted by the disciples of Schoenberg, and were very much in line with the functionalism that dominated the arts in Sweden during the decade 1930–40.

At the same period Rosenberg's early interest in church music renewed itself in the first *Sinfonia da chiesa*. His choral works on religious subjects belong to a later phase; they include the Christmas cantata, *Den heliga natten* (1935), the oratorio-symphony *Johannes uppenbarelse* ('The Revelation of St. John'), and another work in similar form, *Ortagårdsmästeren* ('The Master of the Garden') (1944), which seems to draw upon early impressions in the gardens of Bosjökloster.

These religious works show Rosenberg's earlier preoccupation with abstract forms beginning to yield to an interest in literary subjects. He wrote incidental music for a series of revivals of Greek tragedies and for plays by contemporary Swedish authors. Two operatic works, *Resa till Amerika* ('Journey to America') (1932) and *Marionetter* (1937) preceded a more ambitious score based on Atterbom's *Lycksalighetens Ö.*[1] The ballet *Orfeus i sta'n* illustrates Rosenberg's capacity for absorbing exotic elements. The title ('Orpheus in town') refers to the group of statuary outside Stockholm's chief concert hall, and in the ballet Orpheus seeks Eurydice among the traffic and entertainments of a sophisticated modern capital, much of the musical colour being borrowed from transatlantic jazz.

Two of Rosenberg's symphonies, the fourth and fifth, have already been mentioned as containing elements from oratorio. In the fourth symphony (*The Revelation of St. John*) two parallel texts are used: one from the last book of the Bible, the other a set of seven poems by Hjalmar Gullberg, which are set as a commentary for semi-chorus. In 1948 Rosenberg completed another large-scale scriptural work, an opera-oratorio based on Thomas Mann's *Joseph and his brethren*.

Among the more important abstract works of Rosenberg's maturity are the concerto for stringed instruments (1946) whose middle movement contains one of the composer's rare quotations of folk-tune, taken from a Lapp song. The fifth and sixth string quartets (1949 and 1953) make an interesting comparison with the corresponding numbers in Stenhammar's series of

[1] See page 88.

quartets; the line of ancestry is apparent, but also the impact of modern Viennese methods of construction. Rosenberg begins his sixth quartet with a monologue for the first violin, said to be derived from an earlier sonata:

Reproduced by permission of Nordiska Musikförlaget, Stockholm.

Among Hilding Rosenberg's generation of modern Swedish composers Gösta Nyström (b. 1890) is perhaps the most talented. The son of a schoolmaster and organist in Dalarna, he soon attracted attention not only by his fine singing voice and his brilliant piano improvisations, but also through his gifts as a painter, and his student days in Copenhagen and Paris were divided between the two arts. For twelve years he worked in Paris, moved among progressive French, Italian, and Scandinavian painters and among musicians of various contemporary schools, including D'Indy, who was one of his teachers, Debussy, Ravel, *Lex Six*, Stravinsky, and Schoenberg. Impressionism interested him, both in painting and in music, and his earliest works written in Paris belong to that school; most of them are no longer in existence, but among those that survive are two symphonic poems, *Ishavet* ('The sea of ice'), dedicated to the explorer Amundsen, and *Babelstorn* ('The tower of Babel'), besides an orchestral suite and a symphony that was later revised.

The concerto grosso for strings and the second symphony (*Sinfonia breve*), written in Paris between 1929 and 1931, mark a stage of greater independence and contrapuntal freedom, and an increasing grasp of the larger forms that develops still further in the concertos for viola and for 'cello and the third symphony (*Sinfonia espressiva*) (1935). This has been called a crescendo symphony from its plan, which is distributed over four movements : first, a rhapsodical introduction, metrically free, starting with two violins and gradually adding instruments up to a *tutti* when the process is reversed, after which the movement becomes more animated; the other movements are an *allegro scherzando*—a brilliant *tour de force* for strings, woodwind and horns; a passacaglia on a plainsong-like theme, with trumpets added to the orchestra; and a finale (*allegro risoluto*) for which the trombones have been held in reserve.

As Hilding Rosenberg is inspired by the imagery of the garden, so is Gösta Nyström by that of the sea. In 1948 he wrote a set of five songs with orchestra, all to poems by various authors dealing with aspects of the sea. They are impressionistic miniatures, original and striking, especially in the Phrygian tonality of *Havets visa* ('Song of the sea') to Hjalmar Gullberg's words. In the following year he completed a commission from the Swedish radio to compose a sea symphony; this was written at Capri, entitled *Sinfonia del Mare*, and inscribed with a dedication 'to all sailors on the seven seas'. This work is designed impressionistically, beginning and ending with a tenuous, level 'horizon' of sound, which encloses a stormy allegro in the midst of which there is a lull while a woman's voice recites the sea poem *Det enda* ('The only one').

With Lars-Erik Larsson (b. 1908) we arrive at the middle generation of contemporary Swedish composers. Larsson, a native of Skåne who began his studies in Stockholm under the composition teacher Ellberg, wrote his earliest works in a romantic idiom, which was modified by further experience in Vienna and Leipzig and by coming into contact with the work of Alban Berg and Paul Hindemith. When he returned to Sweden in the 1930s it was as an exponent of the cosmopolitan neo-classical school. One of the first of his important works to attract international attention was the sinfonietta for strings performed at the I.S.C.M. Festival at Florence in 1934. In the same year the popular concerto for saxophone and string orchestra appeared, and has become the first of a complete series of useful short works for various solo instruments with orchestra. Larsson has endeared himself to amateur performers not only by these *concertini* but also by the classic simplicity of the serenade for strings (1934) and, above all, through his cantata *Den förklädd Gud* ('The disguised god') for recitation, soloists and chorus with orchestra, which had its origin in a poetry programme with music for radio. The text, a poem by Hjalmar Gullberg, begins:

> *Ej för de starka i världen men de svaga,*
> *Ej för krigare men Bönder, som ha plöjt*
> *sin jordlott utan klaga,*
> *spelar en gud pa flöjt.*
> *Det är en grekisk saga. . . .*

('Not for the strong in the world, but the weak; not for warriors, but for peasants who have ploughed their plots without complaint, a god plays on the flute. It is a Grecian story.')

The music, introduced by a horn melody of touching beauty, creates an atmosphere of almost sculptural calm. In more recent works by Larsson—the *Missa brevis* for three voices (1954), the *Music for orchestra* (1950), and the violin concerto (1951), there are signs of a development towards greater contrapuntal boldness.

Another composer of the same generation who offers few problems to the listener is Dag Wirén (b. 1905). The natural liveliness of his temperament was enhanced by three years' study in Paris, where his first symphony was written under the guidance of Sabaniev and where a hearing of Honegger's *Le Roi David* was among his most memorable experiences. Since that time his main interest has been in instrumental music, and his fine workmanship, sense of proportion and good-humoured wit have ensured the success of the sinfonietta (1933–4), the 'cello concerto (1936), and the deservedly popular serenade for string orchestra (1936–37). Dag Wirén openly admits that his first desire is to please and entertain; but there is a serious vein running through his geniality that becomes more apparent in the third and fourth symphonies (1940–44 and 1951–52) and in the violin concerto (1946). A quotation from the second movement of the 'cello concerto provides an example of Wirén's elegant, logical style:

*Reproduced by permission
of Carl Gehrmans Förlag,
Stockholm.*

Gunnar de Frumerie (b. 1908) also has a background of study in Paris where Sabaniev and Cortot were his teachers. He is a concert pianist, and his keyboard compositions have an unmistakable Gallic flavour; they include three piano concertos—one, written in 1952, for two pianos—a set of variations and fugue for piano and orchestra, a chaconne for solo piano, and many smaller pieces. Among his orchestral works are a partita for strings and a set of symphonic variations. Gunnar de Frumerie has also composed an opera *Singoalla* (1940) and a ballet, *Johannisnatten*. His songs include a number of settings of poems by Pär Lagerkvist.

A group of younger Swedish composers is linked by the circumstances that all have been pupils of Hilding Rosenberg and that some of them were original members of *Fylkingen*, a society for the performance of music with advanced tendencies which has now been absorbed into the Swedish branch of I.S.C.M. Apart from the style of their master, Rosenberg, diverse influences have made their mark on the group: Carl Nielsen and Sibelius, Bartók and Stravinsky, Schoenberg and Hindemith, besides the revival of ideals and practices from the music of the Renaissance and baroque periods.

Sven-Erik Bäck (b. 1919) and Ingvar Lidholm (b. 1921) have

both drawn inspiration from mediaeval music. Bäck has written motets and a *Sinfonia sacra* for choir and orchestra (1952–3) besides chamber music and a radio opera, *Tranfjädrarna* ('The crane feathers'). Lidholm's three choral pieces entitled *Laudi*, to Latin words from the Old Testament, are written in a modern idiom grounded in sixteenth-century polyphony, with striking experiments in the combination and spacing of unaccompanied voices. Among Lidholm's instrumental compositions a *Toccata e canto* for strings and four woodwind is concisely and effectively written.

The most prolific member of the group, and by far the best known out of Sweden, is Karl-Birger Blomdahl (b. 1916), who entered Stockholm University as an engineering student, but with Hilding Rosenberg's encouragement turned to composition, though he had no real proficiency on any instrument. From that time he set himself the task of obtaining command of a composition technique that would ensure tonal and linear freedom in large-scale works. Among those who gave him advice and support were the Danish choral conductor, Mogens Wöldike, and the Swedish orchestral conductor, Tor Mann. Landmarks in Blomdahl's development have been the production of works at I.S.C.M. festivals, including the string trio at Lund in 1946 and the violin concerto at Amsterdam in 1947. An important choral work, *I speglarnas sal* ('In the hall of mirrors'), based on a sonnet-sequence by the contemporary poet Erik Lindegren, was first heard at Oslo in 1953. Two years earlier the third symphony (*Facetter*) had been performed in Frankfurt.

The boldness and originality of Blomdahl's conceptions, and his flair for creating new patterns of sonority, have caused every major work he writes to be received with close attention, if not always with unanimous approval. Blomdahl's audiences and critics are helped to some extent by his willingness to explain his intentions: for example, he calls the trio for clarinet, 'cello and piano (1955) 'a piece of uncomplicated chamber music of predominantly lyric character'. There is little concession to the lyrical element, however, in the violin concerto, with string orchestra, written in 1946. Here the life of the music is in the ingenuity of the rhythmic permutations, with the solo instrument denied much of its traditional eloquence..

The much publicized and hotly discussed 'space-opera', *Aniara* (1959), fully displayed Blomdahl's eclectic tendencies, being compounded of almost every ingredient in contemporary music: parody of traditional styles, jazz, the pointillisme of Webern, the serialism of Schoenberg and his followers, and sections of electronic recordings introduced for good measure. Whatever may be the ultimate judgement on Blomdahl's work, it is thoroughly representative of the questioning, adventurous spirit of Scandinavian music in the twentieth century. Still younger members of the modern Swedish school, such as Bengt Hambraeus (b. 1928) and Bo Nilsson (b. 1937), are even better known, having attracted notice as determined and radical figures in the *avant-garde* of European composition.

Postscript

The Scandinavian races have been making their contribution to western music since the early Middle Ages. Religious and cultural centres like Roskilde, Vadstena and Nidaros produced hymns and sequences that are of more than academic historical interest as liturgy and chant, and the mediaeval period is rounded off with *Piae Cantiones*, the Swedish-Finnish school hymn book which has permanently enriched the store of popular religious song. The Renaissance court of Christian IV gave protection and encouragement to distinguished executants and composers of many lands. The musical life of the town churches of southern Scandinavia and the cultivation of music in civic and domestic entertainment formed the background of the two baroque composers of talent, Buxtehude and Roman. In the nineteenth century these lands were to yield three symphonists—Berwald, Sibelius, and Carl Nielsen—whose works are known and admired not only throughout Scandinavia, but also throughout the English-speaking countries. The story of European romantic music would be incomplete without the distinctive and not uninfluential figure of Grieg; the repertory of the string orchestra would be much the poorer without the contributions of Wirén, Sibelius, and Grieg again; light music draws upon Lumbye, Halvorsen, and Alfvén; educational music upon Kuhlau, Grieg, Henriques. Every serious singer knows something of Sibelius, Kilpinen, and Grieg, and those who have taken the trouble to study the original languages realize the wealth of Scandinavian song that still awaits exploration.

In modern times, and particularly since the establishment of branches of the I.S.C.M. in the various northern countries, the Scandinavian composer has worked with determination to break down the traditional prejudice, originating in the nineteenth century, against members of what were then considered to be outlying provinces of the European musical state. (This taint of provincialism, it should be noted, never clung to the reputations of the many executive musicians, and especially singers from Jenny Lind onwards, who have made their way from Scandinavian lands to the international opera-stage and concert-platform.) The twentieth-century composer in Denmark, Norway, Sweden and Finland has seldom spent all his studentship at home; he has linked himself in his formative years with the schools of French, German, Austrian, Hungarian and American composition, taking what he needs from them and returning to apply the lessons he has learnt to his native patterns of thought and design.

Different strands in these patterns include a strong belief in the artist's responsibility to the community he belongs to, a sense of satisfaction in grappling with intellectual problems, a love of clear structural logic, in many cases a personal introspectiveness that has its compensation in a keen enjoyment of light, colour, and the use of the arts for pure entertainment. These paradoxes account for some of the liveliest aspects of Scandinavian art and music. Thus, the strain of dourness that has sometimes been noticed in the Swedish temperament finds release in a national flair for brilliant stage production and for wit and colour in dramatic and musical entertainment. The Danish sense of fun breaks through constantly in the older *syngespil*, in the symphonies of Carl Nielsen, and in the lighter compositions of an academic musician like Riisager. Norway has kept closer than her neighbours to the spontaneity of folk music, so that traditional dance rhythms have even now not lost their attractiveness to the heirs of Grieg and Svendsen. While, therefore, the Scandinavian musician of today is equal to the rigours of an I.S.C.M. chamber music festival, and indeed is often to the forefront in adding to them, he does not forget that it is from Scandinavia also that Alfvén's *Midsommervaka*, Dag Wirén's *String Serenade*, and Riisager's *Trumpet Concertino* have gone round the world.

The abundant creative vitality of these small nations, the

liberal artistic policies of their governments, civic authorities, and industrial concerns, the astonishing linguistic virtuosity of their business and professional classes, above all a capacity for becoming citizens of the world—a capacity that has produced, in the wider fields of international relations and social service, a Nansen, a Bernadotte, and a Hammarskjöld—all combine to suggest that their part in the development of the arts, including music, during the second half of the twentieth century will continue to be significant and many-sided.

Appendix 1

The following publications in English will provide further information and commentary on contemporary music in the Scandinavian countries:

Hartog, H. (edr.), *European Music in the Twentieth Century*, London, 1957 (chapter by Wallner, B., 'Modern Music in Scandinavia').

Myers, R. (edr.), *A Guide to Twentieth Century Music*, London, 1959 (chapter by Simpson, R., 'Scandinavian Music').

Alander, B., *Swedish Music*, Swedish Institute, Stockholm, 1956.

Sweden in Music (Musikrevy International), Stockholm and London, 1960.

Hilleström, G., *Theatre and Ballet in Sweden*, Swedish Institute, Stockholm, 1953.

Kragh-Jacobsen, S., *The Royal Danish Ballet*, Copenhagen, 1955.

Helasvuo, V., *Sibelius and the Music of Finland*, Helsinki, 1957.

Lange, K. and Ostvedt, A., *Norwegian Music: a brief survey*, London, 1958.

Appendix 2

JOHANN MATTHESON'S PAMPHLET ON 'SUBTERRANEAN MUSIC IN NORWAY'

One of the oddest of Mattheson's many occasional publications is his pamphlet printed in Hamburg in 1740 under the title:

Etwas Neues unter der Sonnen!/oder/Das Unterirrdische/ Klippen-Concert/in Norwegen/aus glaubwürdigen Urkunden/auf Begehren angezeiget/von Mattheson.[1]

('Something new under the sun: or the subterranean mountain-side concert in Norway, set forth by request from reliable information.')

The 'reliable information' had been supplied by General von Bertouch, a gallant seventy-two-year-old leader of the Danish army stationed in the fortress of Akershus in Christiania and an amateur musician of whom Mattheson thought well enough to give him an entry in his *Ehrenpforte*. Bertouch sent Mattheson two accounts of the hearing of supernatural music, both emanating from respectable middle-aged men for whose credentials Bertouch personally vouches. Whatever we are to make of the stories, they provide interesting evidence of the background of folk-lore that coloured the lives of Norwegian town-dwellers, as well as peasants, at this period.

The first story is related by Hinrich Meyer, a town musician of Christiania, whom Bertouch probably encountered as a regular or occasional member of the officers' band at Akershus.

[1] See Plate XV.

Meyer recalls an experience of his boyhood in 1695, when he was an apprentice musician in Bergen:

Just before Christmas we were rehearsing the music for the festival days. It was customary for a peasant to come every Saturday with milk and butter for my master, Paul Kröplin of Bergen; and while the peasant was waiting for the money for his wares he stood and listened intently to our rehearsal. My master said jokingly to him: 'You can't have any money for your butter and milk today, because you've heard enough to pay you.' 'Strike me,' said the peasant, 'if I don't hear much better, every Christmas eve, a little way from my place, right inside the cliff . . . and if the gentlemen like to come up this evening (it was Christmas Eve) they will find that I've been telling the truth.'

After the peasant had gone, and when the practice was over . . . it was decided to go to the place agreed upon. And so it was; just before the bell struck midnight, the peasant appeared and told us it was time to go to the mountain. I had to go with them and carry a bottle of brandy, for it was very cold. After we had been sitting for a quarter of an hour by the mountain, the Cantor, the Organist, and my master, the Town Musician (Stadtmusikant) got impatient and asked the peasant how much longer they had to sit there. He begged them to have a little more patience.

Soon afterwards the sound of music was heard in the mountain, as if close to us. First a chord was struck, and then a note was given for the instruments to tune to. Then followed a prelude on the organ, and after that a performance duly took place with voices, cornetti (Zincken), sackbuts (Posaunen), violins and other instruments, without the least sign of any visible agency. When we had been listening for a long time, the Organist grew so excited about these invisible musicians and subterranean virtuosi that he exclaimed: 'Hey! If you are from God, let us see you; but if you are from the Devil, make an end of it.' Immediately there was silence; the Organist fell down as if he had had a stroke, foaming at nose and mouth. In such a condition we carried him into the peasant's house and put him to bed . . .

What I have written here is the honest truth, and the tune (printed on the title page) is the one I heard myself in the cliff, near the town of Bergen in Norway; I heard it with my own ears, and have remembered it clearly ever since: witness my hand.

The second narrative, translated from the Danish, came from C. Barth, who describes himself as 'Obrist-Wachtmeister von der Infanterie, auch Platz-Major de Festung Aggerhus'— another veteran even less likely to be credulous, one would have thought, than Stadt-Musikant Meyer or General Bertouch himself; but his discursive reminiscences of his boyhood forty-four years earlier, again in the neighbourhood of Bergen, are full of lively descriptions of the subterranean dwarfs and their mode of life, and of their music which the old soldier had heard, along with 'many other persons, on jews' harps (Mundharffen), langeleiks (Langelög), fiddles, trumpets, and a particular kind of song with human voices, which could not however be understood, but sounded like a halting folk-dance (ein gelalleter Hirtentanz).'

To these stories General Bertouch added a few comments of his own. Similar happenings in Norway, he asserts, could be vouched for by pastors and army men; the common factor appeared to be that the 'concerts' were usually heard on Christmas Eve by anyone who happened to be near the rock-face. He makes another reference to Norwegian tunes played on the *langeleik*, which mystifies Mattheson who has never heard of the instrument before. Finally he appeals to the age of reason (here Mattheson quotes the General's original French):

> Vous autres Philosophes examinez ce Prodige; faites l'imprimer; ditez en vos sentimens publiquement. Pourquoi ce Concert se fait il presque toujours a Noel? Ces Musiciens des montagnes pourquoi ne font-ils du mal a personne, quand on les laisse en repos? Y a-t-il de la Musique dans l'Enfer? je crois, qu'il n'y a la que des hurlemens & du grincement de dents. Vous aurez dans la suite, Monsieur, plusieurs avantures surnaturelles de nos quartiers, desquelles non plus que de celles-ci les habitans du Païs ne soucient gueres . . .

Mattheson repeats the challenge to a sceptical and scientific age:

> I marvel that there are people who bother about the inhabitants of the Moon, when there are creatures on our

own planet of whose nature and character we are almost ignorant.'

He concludes with an adroit puff for his own *Ehrenpforte* as a source of useful information.

The melody printed on the title-page, from the manuscript of Stadt-Musikant Meyer, is identifiable as a fiddle-tune for the Norwegian dance known as the *Halling*: its simplicity hardly tallies with the elaborate 'concert', with voices and several types of baroque instruments, that are mentioned in Meyer's account. It is curious that the professional musicians thought they heard instruments like those they themselves practised, whereas the other narrative, obviously a memory of a peasant childhood, refers to folk-music instruments. A possible explanation of both stories is that the listeners were the victims of practical joking on the part of *Hardingfele* players, whose instruments with their chordal tuning and polyphonic style of performance might, under suitable conditions, create the illusions described.[1]

---

[1] Strong evidence for this explanation is given by Arne Bjørndal in *Norsk Folkemusikk*, Bergen, 1952, pp. 93 seq., where the personages named in Meyer's story are identified.

Index

(The more important books and articles mentioned in the text and notes have been added in brackets after their authors' names)

175

CORRIGENDA AND ADDENDA

page 24, line 3. For *cathedral* read *church (later cathedral)*.

page 30, first music example, second score: add quarter-note rest in bar 1.

page 35, paragraph 2, line 5. For *Åbo University* read *Rostock University*.

page 35, paragraph 3, line 2. For *nearly* read *more than*.

page 36, paragraph 2, line 1. For *intentions* read *intention*.

page 37, paragraph 2, line 2. After *St. Olaf* insert reference to footnote which should read: *Or, more probably, Archbishop Olaus Magnus (d. 1460)*.

page 37, paragraph 3, line 15. For *Fœgsel* read *Faengsel*.

page 44, paragraph 1, line 11. For *have survived* read *has survived*.

page 44, paragraph 2, line 6. For *unpublished* read *published*.

page 48, footnote 1. For *Søro* read *Sorø*.

page 49, 8 lines from end. For *Geistliche Concerten* read *Kleine geistliche Conzerte*.

page 51, paragraph 1, lines 3-4. Delete the words *The Stormaktstid*.

page 51, paragraph 1, last line. For *Förfaras* read *Förfäras*.

page 54, paragraph 2, line 3. For *Skåra* read *Skara*.

page 55, paragraph 2, line 4. For *Storkyrke* read *Storkyrka*.

page 55, paragraph 3, line 6. For *Riddarsholmskyrke* read *Riddarholmskyrka*.

page 56, line 13. For *Fadar vår* read *Fadher wår*.

page 59, paragraph 1, last word. For *Frihetstid* read *Frihetstiden*.

page 62, paragraph 2, lines 4-5. Insert footnote 1 which should read: *Some grounds exist for claiming Oldesloe, in Holstein, as Buxtehude's birthplace. This region was then under Danish rule.*

page 64, footnote 5. Add: *A standard work is Sørensen, S. Diderich Buxtehudes Vokale Kirkemusik, 2 vols., Copenhagen, 1958.*

page 68, line 12. For *Emmanuel* read *Emanuel*.

page 73, paragraph 2, line 2, and page 74, paragraph 2, line 1. For *Charlottenburg* read *Charlottenborg*.

page 76, paragraph 2, line 12. For *a new opera house* read *a new Royal Academy for the promotion of declamation and music*.

page 77, paragraph 1, line 6. For *Musikhogskolen* read *Musikhögskolan*.

page 77, paragraph 2, line 1. For *John* read *Johan*.

page 77, paragraph 2, line 5. For *he wrote Cora och Alonzo* read his *Cora och Alonzo was performed.*

page 78, paragraph 2, line 2. For *sångspelar* read *sångespel.*

page 78, paragraph 2, line 6. For *a sångspel* read *an opera.*

page 78, paragraph 2, lines 9-10. For *similar works* read *sångspel.* For *Gustav Vasa i Dalarna* read *Gustaf Ericsson i Dalarna (1784).*

page 79, line 2. For *1795* read *1797.*

page 79, line 8. For *Youth and madness* read *Youthful madness.*

page 82, paragraph 2, line 7. For *1838* read *1828.*

page 82, footnote 1. For *1850* read *1825.* For *1851* read *1831.*

page 83, main paragraph, 5-6 lines from end. For *Sångar* read *Sånger* in both cases.

page 84, music example. For *regnbåge* read *regnbågen;* for *Sömnes* read *Sömnens;* for *ögor* read *ögon;* for *sukkar* read *suckar.*

page 89, paragraph 3, line 13. For *Bergreen* read *Berggreen.*

page 89, paragraph 3, line 15. For *1870* read *1871.*

page 90, line 2. For *of* read *og.*

page 90, paragraph 3, line 4. For *Jorgen* read *Jørgen.*

page 93, footnote 1. For *1830* read *1880.*

page 95, paragraph 3. Last sentence should read: *The mechanism of a related instrument, the hjulgiga, with . . .*

page 97, line 4. Delete reference to *Kellgren.*

page 98, paragraph 1, line 11. For *1677* read *1678.*

page 98, paragraph 1, line 13. For *Aandeligt* read *Aandelige.*

page 99, paragraph 2, 5 lines from end. For *in* read *i.*

page 103, paragraph 1, line 15. For *allows* read *allowing.*

page 104, last line but one. For *Rikaard* read *Rikard.*

page 104, footnote 1. For *Ackland* read *Acland.*

page 105, line 9. For *Rikaard* read *Rikard.*

page 106. paragraph 3. line 2. Delete the name *Hagerup.*

page 107, paragraph 2, lines 3-6. Insert full stop after the name *A. O. Vinje,* and delete the remainder of the sentence.

page 122, paragraph 2, last sentence. This should read: *This was Asger Hamerik (1843-1923), brother of the musicologist Angul Hammerich and father of the composer Ebbe Hamerik (1898-1951).*

page 122, footnote 1. For *The definitive biography* read *A much fuller biography* and continue the footnote as follows: *A more recent study of Grieg's earlier years is Schjelderup-Ebbe, D. Edvard Grieg 1858-1867 (Oslo and London, 1960).*

page 124, paragraph 2, line 6. For *Et Folkesaga* read *Et Folkesagn.*
page 126, paragraph 1, 3 lines from end. For *Hornemann* read *Horneman.*
page 127, paragraph 1, line 6. For (*b. 1881*) read (*1881-1955*).
page 127, paragraph 2, line 5. For *Nehti* read *Neiti.*
page 129, footnote 1. Add to bibliography: *Layton, R. Sibelius (London, 1965).*
page 132, paragraph 1, line 9. For *cold water* read *spring-water (källvatten).*
pages 136 and following. Since this chapter and the two following were written, a mass of information and criticism relating to all the Scandinavian countries has become available in Wallner, B. *Vår tids musik i Norden*, Stockholm, 1968.
page 137, paragraph 2, line 10. For *Galdreslatten* read *Galdreslåtten.*
page 139, paragraph 2, line 1. For (*1894*) read (*1894-1969*).
page 140, paragraph 2, line 3. For *a symphony (1946) and a piano concerto (1950)* read *two symphonies and a piano concerto.*
page 141, paragraph 2, line 1. For *Cimitière* read *Cimetière.*
page 142. To end of this chapter add: *Since the war the Norwegian national-romantic tradition has yielded considerably to the exponents of contemporary European styles. Representatives of this tendency include Finn Mortensen (b. 1922) and Arne Nordheim (b. 1931).*
page 143, paragraph 1, line 7. For *1890* read *1892.*
page 144, paragraph 2, last line but one. For *Qartsiluni* read *Qarrtsiluni.*
page 144, paragraph 4, line 5. For *1904* read *1908.*
page 148, paragraph 1, line 9. For *1934* read *1924.*
page 151, paragraph 2, lines 1 and 4. For *Aare* read *Aarre.*
page 152, paragraph 3, line 5. For *Ilusia* read *Illusia.* Before last line of this page, add the following: *During the second half of the twentieth century Joonas Kokkonen (b. 1921) has emerged as one of the leading figures in Finnish music, succeeding Uuno Klami as a member of the Finnish Academy. The most important part of Kokkonen's output is in the fields of chamber music and symphonic composition. His style is traditionalist rather than revolutionary, but is little indebted to Finnish national-romanticism. Strongest among his formative influences appear to be Bartók and the Sibelius of the Fourth Symphony.*
page 152, 5 lines from end. For *Eino* read *Einojuhani.*
page 154, line 2. For *Konstforeningen* read *Konsertföreningen.*

CORRIGENDA AND ADDENDA

page 156, line 15. For (*b. 1872*) read (*1872-1960*).

page 158, paragraph 2, line 4. For *1935* read *1936*.

page 158, paragraph 2, line 6. For *Ortagårdmästeren* read *Ortagårdsmästeren*.

page 159, paragraph 2, line 2. For *Gösta Nyström (b. 1890*) read *Gösta Nystroem (1890-1966)*. For *is* read *was*.

page 159, paragraph 2, line 11. For *Lex* read *Les*.

page 160, paragraph 2, line 2. For *Nyström* read *Nystroem*. For *1948* read *1942*.

page 161, paragraph 2, line 5. For *Sabaniev* read *Sabaneiev*. Similarly on page 162, second line after music example.

page 163, paragraph 2, line 2. For (*b. 1916*) read (*1916-1968*).

page 169. Add to Appendix 1 (Bibliography): *Mäkinen, T. and Nummi, S. Musica Fennica. Helsinki, 1965.*

Wallner, B. 'Scandinavian Music after the Second World War.' Musical Quarterly, 1965. no. 1.

Index: corrections to be made as follows:

Date Due

BJJH

PRINTED IN U.S.A.   CAT. NO. 24 161   BRODART